FROM THE AUTHOR OF THE MONSEY-KIRYAT SEFER EXPRESS

ZEV ROTH

10:10

and other timely tales beyond the imagination

TARGUM/FELDHEIM

Published by
Targum Press, Inc.
22700 W. Eleven Mile Rd.
Southfield, Michigan 48034
E-mail: targum@netvision.net.il
http://www.targum.com
Fax toll-free: 888-298-9992

Distributed by
Feldheim Publishers
200 Airport Executive Park
Nanuet, NY 10954
http://www.feldheim.com

Typeset and printed in Israel

Contents

Acknowledgements

I would like to express my gratitude to the Almighty for allowing me to complete my third book.

I would also like to thank

> Yaakov Lavon for his devoted editing

> Yisrael Chaim Mintz for his proofreading

> Michael Silverstein for his wonderful cover

> Rabbi Shmuel Nussbaum א״טילש, Rosh Kollel of Sha'arei Shlomoh where I learn, for reading some of the manuscript and offering suggestions

> Rabbi Zev Leff א״טילש

> My brother, Gary Roth.

A special thank-you to my wife Nomi, for being there when I needed her.

Zev Roth
Rosh Chodesh Tammuz 5763
Kiryat Sefer, Israel

10:10

Leibel was learning in his study when he heard the gentle knock on his door. "What now?" he thought in an instant of impatience, but managed to say politely, "Come in." His wife took a half-step in and said, "Honey, a Mr. Williams is here to see you."

"Who?"

"Williams is the name he gave; he says he's from *Current Legends*."

"Oh, him. Thank you, dear, please show him in." She left and softly closed the door behind her.

Leibel closed his ArtScroll Gemara and stared at the door, waiting anxiously for it to open. He felt his pulse increase. "Could it be? After all these years?"

His wife escorted a man in his mid-forties into the room. Mr. Williams looked haggard, harried, and tired, behind his expensive suit and shiny attaché case. As he came closer, Leibel noticed the rings under his guest's eyes.

Williams approached the desk, extended his hand, and said in a monotone, "Scott Williams, I just arrived from New York."

Leibel reached a hand up from his wheelchair and smiled. "Pleased to meet you. I'm Leibel Gaines. Have a seat, please."

Williams didn't have to be told twice. He almost collapsed into the leather seat in front of Leibel's mahogany desk. As he did, he craned his neck around the study.

"Nice place you've got here."

"I like it."

Williams looked out the window to his right. "You have such a magnificent view. That's Jaffa Gate there, isn't it?"

"I'm more interested in being close to the Western Wall. Is this your first time in David's Village?"

"Actually, it's my first trip to Israel. I'm still jet lagged, but my schedule doesn't include time for rest. I came specially to speak to you."

Leibel lifted his palm in pretended ignorance. "Me? About what?"

Williams let out a sigh that said "I hope this won't be too difficult." After another look out the window he squared his sagging shoulders and addressed his subject. "Mr. Gaines, I'm the co-founder of a website called *Current Legends*. What we do is examine any legend or myth that's being told in our society today, and try to track it down to reality, or else to demonstrate that it's a fantasy. By now we've successfully traced the origin of all sorts of common beliefs, and the reasons behind many popular customs. You may have seen some of our findings; they've been released in a series of books. Perhaps you've seen our new cable TV show, or the website?"

"No, I don't have a television, and I don't use my Internet connection for those sorts of things."

"Oh —." This one was a peculiar customer, no mistake about it. "Well, we just did something that may interest you. We did a full report of how Secretary of State Colin Powell learned to speak Yiddish!"

2

Leibel smiled. "You know, I read all about that in a book I bought recently, *The Monsey-Kiryat Sefer Express.*"

"Yes, we quoted from that book on our program. Now, what I'm here for today is to ask you about a phenomenon that's been around for close to thirty-five years."

"Thirty-five years, you say?" said Leibel, tension and surprise mingling in his voice.

"Yes; our team has done research and conducted interviews, and in the end we were told that you're the one I need to speak with."

Leibel looked more dismayed than shocked. He pointed to his chest: "Me?" He hesitated. This man obviously knew. But Leibel really, really didn't want to talk about it. "What would I know?" he protested, but he knew the charade wasn't going over.

Williams sighed again and looked down for a moment. It was going harder than he'd hoped for. He looked up and said, "We want to know something about advertisements for watches."

Leibel put on his best thoughtful look as he raised one eyebrow. "Watch ads?" he queried blandly.

Williams leaned forward. "Mr. Gaines, we have been asked by many of our site visitors why, in every ad, the hands of the watch are always on the same time: ten minutes past ten."

So he did know. All the same, Leibel did *not* want to talk about it. "Is that so?"

"Yes, and the amazing thing is the universality of the phenomenon. With very few exceptions, in every ad for every brand of watch for the past thirty-five years, the minute hand is on the two and the hour hand on the ten."

Leibel could only think that he must go on stonewalling this inquisitive stranger. Maybe he'd go away. "Oh, surely it can't be so universal as all that."

"But it is," countered Williams. "Just let me open this week's magazines." He lifted his attaché case onto Leibel's desk, opened the latches, and grabbed a stack of magazines out. "This one I picked up in the airport," he muttered as he placed the first one in front of Leibel. "See for yourself. Here's an ad for a Cartier — the hands are at 10:10." He flipped some pages. "Look, here's one for a diamond-studded Brequet, probably sold for over two thousand dollars — also at 10:10." He flipped a few more pages. "Here's a Timex, going for under seventy-five dollars, also 10:10! Care to see any of the others? Or is this something you already know about?"

Leibel ignored the last comment. Instead he thumbed solemnly through the pile of magazines. Williams stood over the desk and looked on intently.

At every ad, Williams stopped and pointed. "Here's one for a Citizen—the hands are at 10:10." Leibel turned more pages until Williams stopped him. "Here—Patek Phillipe, also at 10:10." Leibel picked up a two-month-old *Newsweek* and turned a few pages. When he came to a watch ad he held it closely to his eyes for a few moments. "Well," he drawled, "if you look closely at this one for Raymond Weil, the hands are on 10:08, not 10:10."

Williams shook his head and said, "If you were wearing that watch and someone asked you what time it was, you'd say 10:10, not 10:08, isn't that right?"

4

Leibel barely nodded as he quickly picked up another magazine. There should be an ad for a Swatch somewhere —yes, on this page. He put on an excited look and said, "Hey, here's one that isn't at 10:10!"

Williams was undeterred. "I didn't say the rule applied to every single ad. There are single exceptions, but the phenomenon does occur in almost all instances.

"What's even more interesting is that just recently we've noticed a few companies dropping 10:10 and replacing it with a different time. Perhaps you can let me know what's going on?"

Williams stopped and stared at Leibel for a few moments. The smart thing, thought Leibel, was to protest "How would I know what's going on?" But somehow the words wouldn't come out. He looked at the ceiling and thought. No, he just couldn't talk about it. Hurriedly he stuttered out, "Maybe it's just those issues you brought."

Williams coolly replied, "It's like that in any magazine. Besides, this phenomenon isn't limited to printed media. But let me show you." Glancing over at Leibel's computer, he continued, "Would you mind if I go on-line for a moment?"

Leibel nodded his approval, turned his computer on, and entered his Internet password. Williams came around and hunched himself over the desk next to Leibel. "First let's go to rolex.com," he decided, typing the name on the keyboard. A few moments later, when the site came up, Williams said triumphantly, "Take a look! All the watches are at 10:10." Before Leibel could answer, Williams pushed a few more keys and announced, "Here, this is omegawatches.com. Every watch is set to 10:10." A few more keys and he continued, "Here's an expensive watch site, movado.com. See what time the watches are all at?"

"Maybe it's just those sites?" suggested Leibel, with a hint of desperation in his voice.

"Try any website," countered Williams inflexibly. "It's usually the manufacturer's name, as you undoubtedly know, followed by 'dot-com.' Just go and look: the watches pictured are almost always on or close to the time 10:10."

Leibel shook his head back and forth for a few moments, thinking fast, then faked a smile. "Oh... in advertising, that's what we call symmetry."

Williams opened his eyes wide and asked skeptically, "Symmetry?"

"Yes. Photographers feel that having the hands placed in that fashion shows the watch in a favorable balance. That's really all there is to it."

Williams quickly replied, "If that's so, why aren't any of them set to 1:50? That would give the same symmetry. Another thing: wouldn't each watch manufacturer want his product to look different from the others? Isn't that what advertising is all about, to make your product stand out from the rest? So why are all watches shown in the same pose?"

Leibel persisted, "It's really nothing. The watch just looks nice that way."

Suddenly Williams leaned forward, placed his hands on the desk, and said forcefully, "Mr. Gaines, stop toying with me. My research team have gone thoroughly into this phenomenon. We have reviewed watch ads published over the past thirty-five years. This pose appears in almost every ad, from every company, in every magazine, in every country. It doesn't matter if it's a five-dollar watch or a twenty-five-thousand-dollar one. It doesn't matter if it's a man's Cartier, a woman's diamond-studded Daniel Roth, or a kid's Mickey Mouse watch. The hands on every watch, everywhere, are always on or near the same time—10:10. There's no parallel for this in all of advertising history. I'm here to find out why!" Williams was almost shouting.

Leibel scoured back in his chair. He said softly, "Why do you ask me?"

"You were once the CEO of Barker and Carbo, weren't you? The kings of Madison Avenue, that had most of the major watch accounts thirty-five years ago. This business all started while you were there, isn't that right?"

"...Yes."

"And my people tell me you were the one responsible for it. You must have had a reason. Something happened at ten minutes past ten, right?" Silence.

"Those numbers mean something. What do they mean?"

"...It's like I told you, the watch just looks nice that way."

Williams rolled his eyes and took a deep breath. He had hoped it wouldn't be so difficult. "I didn't want to resort to this, Mr. Gaines, but you leave me no choice."

"Resort to what?" said Leibel apprehensively.

"You aren't the first advertising executive I've spoken to. I know what went on at that convention."

Leibel raised his eyebrows in shock. How did Williams

know about that? He parried with an innocent-sounding "Which convention?"

"The one in Geneva."

Leibel suddenly stared down at his desk. Was the man shaking? Williams wondered. Relentlessly he went on, "I am going to get to the bottom of this one way or another. If you won't help me, I'll have to publish the bits and pieces I've heard from others. I've got just enough to make an article.

"I'd hate to do that, though. Frankly, a number of the stories I've heard are contradictory. There are not so many people alive today from a convention that took place thirty-five years ago, so much of what I got is second-hand recollections and conjectures. I came to you to get the real story."

Leibel sat motionless, staring out in space a few moments. His shoulders slumped as he turned his wheelchair away from Williams, until he faced the window overlooking Jaffa Gate. He was lost in thought for a few moments, then abruptly turned around again and faced his guest. At that moment Williams knew he'd cracked his man open.

Leibel gave a slight smile and said in a soft tone, "All these years it was a secret among the watch manufacturers and their advertisers. Whenever I was asked, I gave them the symmetry answer."

Williams broke into a grin. Sure enough, he was about to get his story.

"If you're going to print it anyway," Leibel began hesitantly, "I think it's crucial you get the story straight. If the Jewish people knew why every watch is set to 10:10, it could change the way they view the world. It could accomplish great things." Leibel looked excited. Forgetting with whom he was speaking, suddenly he lifted his arms and exclaimed, "It could even help bring the Mashiach!"

Williams didn't know what that last bit meant, but it was clear he'd run down his quarry. Finally, some answers! He opened his attaché case once more and took out a Walkman. Placing it on the desk in front of Leibel, he put as much compassion as he could into his voice as he murmured, "I hope you don't mind if I tape this. Please, start from the beginning."

Leibel heaved a sigh and said softly, "All right.... The beginning. Where is that?... You know, I wasn't always religious the way I am today."

"So I'm told."

"I was raised in an Orthodox home by immigrant parents, but like most of my generation, I dropped religion to chase the American dream. I forgot about living a Jewish life in favor of what I thought was 'the good life.' I didn't even call myself Leibel any more. My name back then was Larry.

"I remember in 1967 when my secretary buzzed me and said I had a call on line 3. The other party sounded peeved, she said...."

"Mr. Gaines, Mr. Curtis says it's urgent."

"I can't stand her squeaky voice," I thought as I reached for the phone, and brusquely told her through the intercom, "Okay, I got it."

I picked up the phone and swiveled my leather chair so I could see out the glass window, where I stared at the Chrysler building.

I put on my cheeriest voice and said, "Bob? How are you?"

Curtis didn't return the greeting. "What's this we hear about your latest harebrained vacation plans?"

I was taken aback. "Er, what about it?"

"Another high-thrill jaunt, Larry? Mountain climbing in the Sierra Nevadas this time, I understand."

"Actually, I'm going to spend two weeks backpacking on a few of the peaks in California. I've been planning it for several months."

"Is that a way for an advertising executive to spend his time off?" I couldn't help noticing how annoyed Curtis sounded. Well, he was annoying me, too. I replied curtly, "What's it to you where I vacation?"

"What's it to me? How do I explain this to the shareholders, after what happened to Watson?"

"That could've happened to anyone."

"I realize that, but the board members are fed up with you risking your life for a thrill. We have millions invested in plans that require you to be around to run this agency. We can't afford to have you taking risks like this."

"Watson was just unlucky...."

"I'm the unlucky one, Larry. How do you think it feels when you get a call on Sunday afternoon to come to the hospital to identify a body? And it's the body of someone you've known for fifteen years? Not to mention that I was the one who had to break the news to his wife and kids.

I don't feel like doing that again."

I scooted my chair forward and put my elbows on the desk. Bent over, my hand on my forehead, I thought. How could I make him understand? I searched for the right words, but none came to my head. I didn't realize I was taking so long until I heard Bob again.

"Hello? Larry? Larry! Are you still there? Are you listening to me?"

I couldn't stand it. I blurted out, "Do you know I'm here from six in the morning until midnight most of the week? Do you know how many hours I sit here in this office keeping the customers happy?"

"Larry, I...."

"'You have to be available at all hours,' the board tell me. 'You're the CEO, and we have watch ads running all over the world at all hours of the day. You have to be there.' Bob, sometimes I put in twenty-hour days! The crisis last month, trying to save the Citizen account, kept me thirty hours without sleep. I need a break sometimes! Is that asking too much?"

There was a pause, until Bob broke it. "Nobody says you can't have a vacation. Its just these risks you take with your life. You've got us worried...."

"I'm not the type to sit on a beach and stare at the waves all day. I need action and excitement. I tried the safari that time just because you asked, but it was a big bore. All I got was a snapshot of a toucan."

"I understand all that, but couldn't you pick something a little safer?"

I sat back in my chair and calmed myself down. "You

know why I go on these adventure trips? I'll tell you. I'm on the verge of cracking from the pressure of this job. Maybe you don't know it, but it's become common for executives to take thrill vacations, and never mind how dangerous. I've gotta tell you, everyone that's done it agrees it's the best thing for your nerves. The jolt of excitement is just what you need to — I don't know what, but when you get back to the office you're ready to face the stress again.

"Besides, I'm taking all the standard safety precautions, and I'm going with a doctor who's done this sort of trip before."

Curtis knew he was licked. He muttered, "Just don't try parachuting like Watson did."

"Skydiving? I tried that years ago. ... Did they ever figure out why his back-up parachute didn't open?"

"All they can say is that it was a nasty accident. Look, Larry, just do me a favor. Take care of yourself."

"I will, Bob. And thanks for your concern."

I hung up the phone, swiveled my chair again and stared out the window. There it was again, the Chrysler building. And Mrs. McBride's squeaky voice once again interrupted my thoughts: "Mr. Gaines, Dr. Newfeld on line 2." I smiled, twirled my chair around to my desk and quickly picked up the phone. "Milo?"

"How are ya, Larry? Can you come over on Saturday? I've gotta show you how to pack. I hope you've been doing that exercise program."

"Sure, every day." I blushed at the lie — I never had time for exercise. Getting some time off for the trip had been tough enough.

That Saturday I went to visit my long-time friend, Dr. Milo Newfeld, to work out the final details of the trip. As soon as I arrived Milo escorted me down to the basement stair. As usual, Milo had trouble finding the light switch in the dark, but in a moment the narrow wooden staircase was washed in dull light.

We went downstairs and headed for the right corner, where Milo had made a "command center" for his mountaineering trips. His knapsack was lying on a shaky old bridge table. All sorts of items surrounded it — too many, I thought, how could he remember them all? Mess kit, crampons, lines and clips, staffs, parkas, boots for every terrain, extra laces… I noticed a huge first-aid kit. Maps, compasses, blankets, and on the hooks on the wall, spikes and ropes for rock climbing. The bookshelf was full of survival guides and mountaineering manuals.

"The secret," announced Milo, "is to travel light. That's why I asked you to come here today: I want to show you how to pack your knapsack. And first I wanted you to see what I'm bringing." He handed me a typed list.

I took one look at it and scratched my head. At first I thought it was a price list for all the things on the table. Another look, and I realized that the figures weren't prices, it was the weight of each item. I couldn't believe it, though. I blurted out something like, "You *weigh* all these things before you put them in your knapsack?"

Milo replied confidently, "Every one. I used the scale from my office, and for the smaller items I borrowed the scales my pharmacists use to measure dosages."

I scanned over the list, lifted my eyebrows, and said simply, "Impressive." It was. Each necessary item was listed there, with its exact weight to the decimal. I squinted, however, over the listing of contents on the first aid kit. One item "Tehillim — 2 oz." I quickly asked, "Tehillim? That's not what I think it is?"

Milo looked up from reading his atlas, a bit red in the face. "It's the Book of Psalms."

"I know what Tehillim is. Why are you taking that along?" I asked. I couldn't help it, the words came out accusingly.

Milo looked a bit flustered. He groped for an excuse a few moments, then I could see him deciding that he'd have to tell the truth. "I lost a patient in surgery a few months ago...."

"So?"

"I was close to him. I really thought he might pull through. I had just administered a new treatment when suddenly his vital signs went haywire. Before I could do anything, it was too late.

"When I realized he was gone, I was in a daze. I went home, but I didn't know what to do. Read a medical journal? Put on a TV comedy? A round of golf? None of those things could do it for me. I wandered around the house, and I came into this room. That's where I found my grandmother's beat-up book of Tehillim. I don't know what came over me. I remembered her carrying that book around with her wherever she went. ... She used to read from it all the time, you know.

"When she passed away a few years ago, I inherited a

few of her books. I didn't really know what to do with them, so I shoved them on the end of this shelf." Milo pointed to a few worn spines with Hebrew lettering, over at the end of his mountaineering bookshelf.

"Well, when I wandered in that day, I spied that book sitting at the end of the shelf, and I remembered Grandma. I don't quite know what I remembered, but it was in my mind. Suddenly I figured, "Why not?" and took the book down. I still remembered some Hebrew from my Bar Mitzvah. I could read the words. Even though I didn't know what I was saying, after a few minutes or so I felt a lot better. I don't know, maybe it was a feeling that Grandma, or somebody, was listening to me. Maybe just that made me feel better."

"Very nice, but why are you taking it with us?" I asked. Now I was just bewildered. I really didn't like hearing stuff like this.

Milo only smiled in embarrassment. "Well, after that — experience — I started keeping Grandma's Tehillim in my first-aid kit." Lovingly he picked up the old book and stowed it in the first-aid box. Then he looked puzzled, and suddenly turned to me and asked, "How do you know what a Tehillim is?"

"'Know what it is'? What do you mean? I've said a lot of Sefer Tehillim on a lot of occasions. Uh, I guess I never mentioned that I went to Orthodox schools until I was a teenager."

Milo stared at me with a blank look on his face. "I never knew you were from a religious background. You still go to shul?"

"Twice a year."

"Same with me. Any religious relatives?"

"Nope. Yourself?"

"Just one uncle who lives upstate. He got most of the other religious articles. He's the one most like my grandmother."

Milo shook himself, then pulled down an atlas (one of many) and opened it. "I wanted to show you this map. It details the terrain of three peaks: Middle Palisades, Bishop's Pass, and Mount Sill. They're among the tallest in the Sierra Nevadas. I say we go for those three, and maybe one or two more."

I lifted his eyebrows. "Three of them? How many are there altogether?"

"Whatsamatter, three's not enough? In all, there are fifteen mountains over fourteen thousand feet, so we should be pretty busy for the two weeks."

A few weeks later we were once again comparing notes and looking at maps, only this time we were in Kennedy Airport. I felt silly — I hoped nobody I knew would see me with my knapsack. I had been through this airport so many times in my executive suit and attaché case; now the knapsack made me feel awkward. As I stood in line to check in, I was shocked when I saw a few others join the line. They all carried the same kind of knapsack that I had, only they were wearing tie-dyed shirts and long, messy hair. Great, now I felt downright foolish. "These hippies," I thought, "are also going to California. If I had a little longer hair, they might think that I'm going with them." I was glad once I'd checked in my luggage and saw my knapsack go on the conveyor belt. I could move away from the others.

Shortly after the plane took off, I was about to open my Wall Street Journal when suddenly the person in the seat in front of me turned around. I saw long black hair and a large peace-symbol medallion dangling from a paisley shirt. "Hey," he said, "I saw you check in with a knapsack. You headed to Frisco?"

"No, actually we're going to do some mountain climbing in the Sierra Nevadas for a couple of weeks."

"Groovy. Sure you don't want to check out the Monterey Pop Festival? The Byrds are gonna be there, and Buffalo Springfield."

"Um, no thanks, we'll stick to our plans."

After an uneventful flight, we got a cab that brought us to a supermarket. The driver waited for us with the meter running while we stocked up on supplies. A few hours later, as the sun was disappearing below the mountain, he dropped us off on a dirt road near the foothills of Middle Palisades. Milo paid the driver extra and told him to pick us up at the same spot two weeks later. "I sure hope that guy remembers to pick us up," I said in surprise, a bit shocked that Milo had trusted a total stranger.

Milo just said, "Did we have a choice? Besides, with these knapsacks we could always hitchhike. We'll say we're going to the Monterey Pop Festival."

"Very funny."

"Let's find a place to set up camp. I hope you plan on getting up early."

"How early?" I asked, as my eyes opened wide.

"Sunrise," he answered nonchalantly.

I gulped. "Come on," I assured myself. "I'm used to putting in long hours at the office, so it shouldn't be too difficult."

After wandering around a bit, we came across a spot that was away from the road and clear of rocks and roots. Milo said, "It's getting dark. This place is as good as any, so let's camp."

Sometimes it got on my nerves that Milo was so organized, so I broke into a grin when Milo took the tent out of his knapsack and half the contents spilled on the ground.

He just grunted, "Gimme a hand." With a bit of fumbling, he unrolled the orange pup tent and the support poles. But when he took his hammer to bang the spikes into the ground, I saw him suddenly make a frantic reach into each pocket of his knapsack, one after the other. "Uh-oh," he yelled, "where are they?"

"Where's what?" I had no idea what was missing.

"The tent spikes! Wait a minute, this is really bad. I carried the hammer and poles, but you were supposed to carry the spikes."

I said quickly, "No, you had them."

Right away we both started searching our knapsacks. Even I realized that the tent couldn't stay up without spikes to hold it to the ground.

I had dumped almost my whole bag out when Milo yelled, "Here they are!" Now that we found the spikes, the tent was up in a few minutes.

We ate some sandwiches we had brought along at

Milo's suggestion, and then crawled into our sleeping bags, exhausted from all the traveling. Within minutes we were both asleep.

True to his word, the next morning at sunrise Milo woke me up. He'd already lit a small fire for breakfast. I sat up in my sleeping bag, wondering for a moment why I had ever agreed to this jaunt. I was used to getting up at dawn for the office, but I'd always feel groggy until my first cup of coffee. This time, oddly, I felt awake after just a minute or two. "Must be the fresh mountain air," I thought.

We took down the tent, and after putting out the fire began to hunt around for a trail marker. After about fifteen minutes we found something that vaguely resembled a trail, and began our ascent.

For the first time since the trip started, I actually had to carry that knapsack up a mountain. Over sixty pounds weighed down on my shoulders while at the same time I climbed a steep path. Only now did I realize how heavy the thing was. By eleven o'clock my shoulders ached.

Around one o'clock we put down some sandwiches and water while sitting on a rock. Then Milo said, "Okay, let's get going. I'd like to be at around six thousand feet by tonight."

I was massaging my shoulders and asked, "what's the rush?"

"I told you, there's a few peaks I'd like to reach."

I took another look at my knapsack. I didn't particularly like the idea of putting it on my back again. When I looked up I was astonished: there stood Milo, knapsack on back and ready to go. Since I had no alternative, I drew on some strength I didn't know I had. I stood up, and with some help from Milo managed to put my knapsack back on. It was so heavy that I blurted out, "How can you carry all that weight and it doesn't bother you?"

Milo smiled, "Oh, this knapsack is nothing. You should see what I carry on the golf course."

"You don't take a golf cart?"

"How do you think I keep in training for carrying this knapsack?"

Toward the end of the day, around six thousand feet above sea level, we were treated to a majestic California sunset. Then, with the darkness descending, once again we realized we'd better set up camp as quickly as possible. As soon as Milo had built a small fire, I hurriedly sat beside it and warmed myself. Looking up at Milo I said, "It sure gets cold here."

"That's because we're high up in the mountains; the dry air up here doesn't hold any heat once the sun goes. Besides, we're not so far from San Francisco — do you know what Mark Twain said about Frisco this time of year?"

"No, what?"

"He said, 'The coldest winter I ever spent was a summer in San Francisco.'"

Suddenly I went rigid. I was sure I heard footsteps. Who could be with us on the mountain? I pointed my flashlight, only to see two shiny eyes stare back at me, then disappear. "What was that?" I puzzled.

"A lynx? A coyote?"

"Milo, you say the most encouraging things. Any more creative ideas like that?" After a few moments of silence I said, "Whatever it is, I hope he doesn't come back."

After a few minutes I calmed down and began to watch the colors of the fire, only to get another jolt. There were footsteps again. Again I used my flashlight, but this time the animal just stared back without moving. I got a closer look at our four-footed visitor, and panicked. "It's a raccoon!" I grabbed a pebble and threw it at him, and watched him run off.

Milo said, "Oh, just a raccoon. He's probably looking for some food. They know that humans frequently leave goodies behind..."

"Shhhh!" I thought I heard it again, this time more of them, and closer. I flashed my light and saw three raccoons not more than fifteen feet away. Milo looked surprised, and asked me, "How come you're getting so worked up over a little raccoon?" I managed to grate out, "They're a lot more dangerous than you think, Milo." After that he stared along with me at our unexpected guests. A few moments later he said thoughtfully, "All right, what do you say we make the fire a little bigger?" He threw in some of the branches he had cut, and the fire grew larger. Now it was so hot that I backed away from it. The raccoons, however, were not scared off. They stayed right there, behind the brush they were hiding in.

At first I thought I was imagining it, but when the sound grew louder chills ran down my spine. An angry growling was coming from the patch of brush. I could hear leaves shaking, and I began to shake myself. I knew it wasn't because I was cold — the fire kept me warm enough. But I had never heard a sound like that before. It was changing now, sounding like a pit bull that had swallowed helium — a high-pitched, screeching growl. I looked at Milo, but with all his mountaineering experience he didn't know what to do. All he could say was, "Raccoons are usually harmless to man." He didn't sound too confident, though. I was scared stiff. "Ever since I read in a book," I told Milo, "that packs of raccoons can outfight a full-grown wolfhound...." Milo gave me a look that said, "I wish you hadn't mentioned this."

"I read it when I was little," I explained, while my voice trembled. "I've been scared of raccoons ever since. I mean, do you know just how big wolfhounds are?"

"Uh, yeah, I do," said Milo. He was obviously thinking that he didn't want to be the one who found out whether a full-grown human could outfight a raccoon pack. I knew what he was thinking, because it was just what I was thinking.

I suggested, "Maybe I should throw them some food."

"No!" yelled Milo. "That will only bring more of them!" Instead he built the fire higher, but the growls and shakings around only got worse over there in the brush. I kept my eyes in that direction, when just to my left I heard more footsteps. My heart was pounding. I jerked around, to see yet another raccoon standing not more than ten feet from me.

I had parachuted, scuba dived in the Caribbean, gone water-ski racing, and most recently been on a safari in Africa. Now, of all times, I felt my heart racing with the beginnings of panic. Thoughts raced wildly through my head. "Those things have really sharp teeth. There's a whole pack of them over there. What if they attack?"

Milo added in a shaking voice, "I don't recall reading in medical journals about raccoon attacks … but who knows? They might have rabies or something." This wasn't helping me. Shaking worse every second, I said plainly, "I don't want to be the first case. Let's get out of here!"

Milo didn't have to be told twice. The two of us quickly took down the tent, packed up the camp, and put out the fire. The eerie darkness only sent my heart beating wildly — I thought the man-eating raccoons would attack at any minute. Just then I heard another growl, and I swear I heard footsteps coming closer. Panic-stricken, I ran, and in the darkness I didn't see a stone in my way.

I tripped over it, and when I put out my hand to stop the fall it landed on a sharp projecting stem. I felt a burning pain in my hand. Did a raccoon just bite me? I wondered feverishly. Now I was down, surely the raccoons would pounce on me any moment. Suddenly I heard myself say some words that I hadn't said in over thirty years: '*ana Hashem hoshi'ah na*, please, God, save me!"

With that, I found the strength to get up and run. Milo was right behind me. Only when we were far away from the growling brush did I stop to clean myself off and take a look at my hand.

Milo examined it with his flashlight. "Only a small cut, not a bite, just a plain puncture. I'll take care of it once we find another campsite."

We walked on for another five minutes or so, and

found a rocky clearing away from the trees. It was a bay in the mountain, backed on three sides by a cliff. "Here's a good spot," said Milo. "If the raccoons come back, they can only come at us from one direction."

I looked at Milo, puzzled. "We're going to sleep on rocks?"

Milo said, "You'd rather sleep near the raccoons? Anyway, let me get a bandage for that cut."

Milo reached in his knapsack, and this time found the first-aid kit right away. As he turned his flashlight on it, for a moment I saw the Tehillim lying at one side. Then Milo took out a bottle of antiseptic and a bandage, and all I could think of was not yelling when he put the stuff on my cut. I always was a baby about antiseptics.

It only took us about twenty minutes to reassemble the tent — there was a small spot of thin soil we found among the rocks. Milo didn't think the tent was really necessary, but I insisted on it as a protection in case any of our friends again came calling. Okay, it wasn't much of a protection, but I had to have something.

We were too riled up to go to sleep right away. I insisted on getting a fire going, in case those raccoons found our new camping spot. But by now, we were both starting to think of the whole episode as pretty funny. "Why do you think they came out now?" I wondered.

Milo said, "These are the first warm days of spring. They're probably hungry, and know that backpackers leave goodies."

"I can see it now," I mused with a crooked grin. "I survive parachuting, a safari, diving and all the rest of my adventures, only to be polished off by a bunch of tiny little raccoons!"

We both laughed, then I got more serious. "When I fell, I was pretty scared. I said a verse I hadn't said in years — I think it's from Tehillim. Mind if I have a look and see if I can find it?"

Milo reached into his first-aid kit, grabbed the old Tehillim, and gave it to me. The minute I touched it, I realized how fragile it was. "I think you ought to get a new one for these trips, Milo," I told him. "This one's not gonna last much longer."

I started to hunt through the brown pages, skimming each chapter. Milo watched with open amazement, and finally asked, "You really know a lot about Tehillim, don't you?"

I felt annoyed without knowing why. "I told you before, I went to a Torah Academy until high school. I used to learn Chumash, Mishnah, all that stuff, and whenever someone was sick we said Tehillim for them."

"So, what happened?" Milo was getting curious. "When did you stop with the religion?"

I wasn't sure if I liked this line of conversation, but I didn't have any excuse not to tell him the truth. "Well, in my second year of high school I transferred to a private school in Dartmouth, and I was one of just a few Jewish students there. I had non-Jewish roommates who went to parties Friday night and football games on Saturday afternoons. I didn't want to be left out, so I sort of dropped everything once I got there. Anyway, it was really difficult to stay religious and keep up with all my studies."

Milo asked, "How did your parents feel when you weren't keeping mitzvos any more?"

I stared into the fire. I didn't talk very often about what happened to my parents. Milo didn't know; hardly anybody knew about it. I almost gave my standard response, "I'd rather not talk about it," but we were on a mountain away from civilization. This time I felt different, as if it wasn't a big deal to confide in him. "My parents weren't around anymore. They both died in a car accident."

Milo rocked back as if he'd been punched. He stared at the fire too, then said quietly, "I'm sorry."

I knew he hadn't meant to open old wounds. "It's still a bit painful," I explained, "but you couldn't be expected to know. That's why, though, I don't talk about it. I guess I was mad at God for taking them both away from me when I was so young.

"After the accident I went to live with my aunt and uncle, but they weren't as religious as my folks were. I guess that's where it started. And then, what with one thing and another, and going to Dartmouth Academy... and well, that was that."

I saw that Milo was as uncomfortable as I was with this conversation. I guessed that in spite of being a doctor, he didn't like to deal with the topic of death. And we'd never talked about Jewish things. I quickly changed the subject. "I keep looking through this Tehillim, but I can't find the verse I said to myself back there."

Milo yawned. For a change, he seemed to be the tired one this evening. I guessed the excitement of the day was catching up to him. He said, "Hang on to the book all you want, just give it back when you're done with it." Milo put out the fire, and headed straight for the tent. I followed behind. Once inside the tent, I started to feel more safe. I shut my eyes, and when I was certain there were no footsteps outside I fell into a deep sleep.

The next morning we woke up at around seven o'clock. After some cookies and coffee we packed up the camp and started off. The trail, when there was one, was twisted, and at times it was very hard to find. We were frequently forced to improvise around boulders and small trees. At times we weren't even sure if we were going in the right direction — not that it mattered, as long as we were going up. But the whole day was a monotonous drag of climbing over rocks, walking on dirt, and stopping frequently to catch our breath.

As we climbed higher, I felt so short-winded that it was as if I had only one lung. Soon we could go no faster than a slow walk, and much of the time we were spending climbing over rocks. Around dusk, I realized I couldn't go any further. "At least there aren't any raccoons up here," I quipped, wondering uneasily if maybe they could live even at this height.

We found a small clearing to make camp, and when I was finally able to sit and rest for a while, I realized two things: my legs ached, and it was cold. My head pounded from the lack of oxygen. Milo made a small fire and cooked some hot dogs, and I was amazed how much I ate. I devoured two whole meals' worth of rations on the spot, and still felt hungry afterwards.

That night, even though I was exhausted from the

climb, I was so light-headed I couldn't sleep. I threw on some clothes, took a few steps outside the tent, and looked up. The sky had more stars than black space between them. I stared in awe for a long time, and gradually, for the first time on this trip, I got a feeling of peace and oneness.

Suddenly I realized that the verse I had said when running from the raccoons was in the Hallel part of Tehillim. For some reason that idea wouldn't leave my head. My thoughts starting whirling around in my head like ice cream in a blender. What had I been doing all these years? I had climbed the ladder to become the head of one of the biggest advertising firms on Madison Avenue. Did I deserve the credit? Who gave me strength, and the will to fight on, to keep going, and to overcome the setbacks? I wasn't so sure any more that "my strength" was really my own. This very day, a pack of tiny creatures had sent me running in terror. That meant I wasn't so mighty as I had thought I was. ... Did I really still have to be so mad at God for taking away my parents?

I didn't know where that last thought had come from, but once it came it wouldn't go away. Eventually I went back to bed, but I didn't sleep very well that night.

The next day was a rerun of the previous, except I felt worse. In the late afternoon we reached fourteen thousand feet, and the summit was in view.

By then my whole body ached, and I was having trouble breathing. Then I made the mistake of looking up. When I saw what we'd have to go through to reach the summit, my jaw dropped. Even Milo stopped and stared at what lay in front of us. The approach to Middle Palisades summit looks like a six-hundred-foot-long football field, made all of slippery stones and boulders; and somebody has taken this field and tilted it up at an eighty-degree angle. The guide books said it didn't require special climbing gear, and I guess it didn't (that was good, since neither of us was trained to use that kind of gear). But we were obviously going to spend the rest of the day scrambling on hands and knees over slick rocks.

I just stood there and didn't budge, because I didn't think I could do it. I was about to suggest to Milo that he could go on if he wanted, but I'd stay put — "maybe the next peak wouldn't be so difficult...." Suddenly Milo interrupted my thoughts. "Let's look around! Maybe there's some kind of trail, or at least an easier way up."

It was getting late; I hoped Milo wasn't considering starting the climb this late in the day. Still, I pushed my body along. We'd been walking around the rocky area for about ten minutes when Milo spotted what looked like a small path. We couldn't know where it led, or even if it was usable, but Milo suggested we give it a go. I said, "I'll wait here, you start up the path for five minutes or so. If you find it's not a trail, I think we'd better camp here and look some more in the morning."

Milo gave a halfway grin and said, "Okay, you take a rest. But I hope you can catch your second wind — I was planning on reaching the summit today." He hopped up onto the rocks and began scrambling up, sometimes on all fours. I watched him until some boulders blocked my view. I took off my knapsack and leaned it against a rock, and took a seat on a boulder.

I sat there and just felt the cold air blowing by. It was clean and sharp, and strangely soothing. I began to feel sleepy, and shut my eyes for a few minutes.

All of a sudden I was being shaken back and forth. My eyes flew open. I felt the whole mountain shake! What was happening? Was I dreaming? I couldn't figure out what was going on. Suddenly I remembered where I was: in California, not far from the San Andreas fault. This was an earthquake, and I was in the middle of it.

The shaking only lasted for a few seconds, then started to settle down. I was about to yell out to Milo when suddenly I heard a rumbling sound. I looked up, and there was a whole mountain-load of rocks tumbling right towards me, getting louder and closer very quickly. Much too quickly for my liking.

I wasn't thinking about Milo any more. My first thought was to run, but where could I go? I saw the rocks coming straight for me, and all I could do was sit there, feeling terrified. I saw the first few pass me by, then I gasped in pain as a big one crashed into my shin, just below my right knee, and pinned me against the rock I was leaning on. I cringed in pain, so bad I couldn't even try to pull my leg out, not that it would've budged. I was trapped. I sat still, terrified, expecting the end to come. Another large boulder would come at me any moment and finish me off. I held my breath.

Then, just as quickly as the rockslide had come, it was gone. I heard the rocks roll past me further down the mountain, and then there was nothing but silence left.

I sat there for a few moments, pinned by the rock that had hit my leg. Finally I began to check my body over. It was still in one piece. I moved my shoulders — sore from carrying the knapsack — and then my hands. Everything was in order. Then I tried to move my leg from under the rock. The pain was so bad I gasped and went limp all over. When I'd caught my breath I tried to push the rock off my leg, but it didn't budge. Too heavy.

Another attempt to move my leg proved that this wasn't a good thing to try. I got a hunch my leg was broken in more than one place. I would need to see a doctor, like Milo... Milo! I screamed for him. "Milo! Are you okay? Milo!" There was no answer. Fearing the worst, I hit the verge of panic. Wildly I tried to pull myself out of the boulder trap; this time I almost fainted, the pain was so strong. I screamed again, "Milo, do you hear me?" I heard only silence.

After a while I managed to think rationally for a few moments. Milo couldn't have gone too far before the quake hit. So why didn't he answer? He might be dead. He might just have gotten a blow on the head. Was he unconscious? Why on earth didn't he answer? I screamed as loud as I could, "Milo? Can you hear me? Anyone? Help!" Again I heard nothing but the sounds of my panic.

I tried to come up with a plan, but quickly realized I was helpless. All I could do was wait for help. At that, my thoughts turned rational again. Help... I had to get help.... With a jolt I realized that the rescue scene didn't look too good. Who knew we were up here? Probably that tremor barely registered on the Richter scale. It only lasted twenty seconds or so. It probably didn't cause any damage below. Why, quakes were a common occurrence in California: this tremor wouldn't even make it into page six of the local newspaper. "Why should anyone look for us?" I thought in despair. "How would they know we're in trouble?"

It was getting dark, and I wished I had a phone in my knapsack. I screamed for help every few minutes, but only got the wind as my answer. I kept hoping that any minute Milo would come down from those rocks and help me get this boulder off my leg. By the time the stars were out it didn't seem likely any more.

Now it was full night, and I could barely see fifteen feet in front of me. If by some miracle help came, they wouldn't be likely to find us in this darkness. I settled down to survive the night, my head churning alternately with stabs of pain and equally uncomfortable thoughts. Maybe this trip wasn't such a great idea after all. Did I really need all this adventure, risking my life for a thrill? Wasn't my life worth more than making sport with? I wondered if I would ever get out of this, if I would ever see my wife and children again.

The night went by in a daze of pain and cold. My knapsack was somehow still leaning where I had left it, and I managed to take out my sleeping bag, unzip it, and cover myself with it. At least I wouldn't freeze. I kept my eyes shut and managed to doze off a few times. The hours passed slowly.

Once the sun came up, I realized I was still alive, and called for Milo a few more times. Still no answer. "Probably dead," I thought groggily, too dazed with pain to take my own words seriously.

I groped around and managed to find some trail mix in the bottom of my knapsack. There were still a few swallows of water in the canteen on my belt. "All the comforts of home," I thought with silent hysteria. "Now if I could only get this rock off my leg...." It almost seemed funny.

But by nine-thirty I was more awake, and getting desperate. My water was all gone and my throat was parched. Maybe I should have rationed it better, but I wasn't exactly thinking straight. I could hardly feel my leg any more, but when I did it took all my strength not to scream with the pain. I didn't see any way out of this.

Suddenly my head cleared and I could think for a moment. I realized with absolute clarity that only God could help me. Things I had learned in my yeshivah days sprang up in my mind like a geyser. I recalled my Rabbis teaching that prayer has the power to accomplish great things. "Just as a soldier wouldn't go out to war without his machine gun, prayer is a Jew's weapon. As long as you can pray, don't give up hope, even if a sword is at your neck."

There was only one problem. What should I say? I didn't remember any more how the words went.

Suddenly I realized I had Milo's Tehillim! I groped feverishly inside my knapsack — there it was. I hadn't really paid attention before to the facing English translation, but now I was glad it was there. I remembered a lot of the Hebrew, but most of the time I said the English, so that I'd know what I was saying. I started at the beginning and just said one Tehillim after another.

By ten o'clock I was in so much pain I could hardly

mumble the words any more. I was so weak that suddenly the Tehillim dropped out of my hands. I stared at it. How could I pick it up, with my leg in this shape? But I knew I couldn't leave it on the ground. Gritting my teeth, I crouched and bent down to pick it up. As I got a grip on it, the pages fell open, and I was shocked by what I read. "He crouches, he bows down, and into his might falls the helpless." I thought I knew what that meant. So this is how it ends?

After I read that verse I couldn't go on any more the way I'd been doing. The charade had to end.

I started letting out all the emotions I'd kept penned in from the time I left for Dartmouth. I sat up as straight as I could, lifted my hands to the heavens, and said out loud the verse I'd read just before I dropped the Tehillim: "שויתי ה' לנגדי תמיד, I have set Hashem before me always." Always keep God in your consciousness, always think about God and what He would say about your actions. That was one of the central points the Rabbis had taught me all those years ago. I made a promise to God: if I ever got out of this alive, I would finally live with this message, and I'd try to spread it to others. I didn't have the foggiest idea how I'd go about it, but I told Him I would take it on if He would only save me.

For the first time in over twenty years, I let out my heart. I spoke to God in ways I never had before. Shutting my eyes to the agony in my leg, for the first time in my life I prayed with everything I had — well, everything I had left. I told God I was sorry I had worked on Shabbos. I'd thought at the time that I had to do it to get ahead, but what good was all my money now? I was willing to learn my lesson.

How long did I sit there, reaching towards Heaven with my arms outstretched? I don't know. I guess it wasn't long, but I was so exhausted, in such pain, I was past even feeling time go by. My eyes fell shut, but my arms stayed stretched up and out — I don't know why or how. I only know that I opened my eyes and looked up through my arms when I thought I heard something. It sounded like a helicopter, and the sound was getting closer and closer. My arms were up already, so I began to wave them frantically. The helicopter seemed to see me right away. It dipped down and then hovered in front of me about fifty feet over my head. I saw the pilot wave to me and give thumbs up, then he flew off.

He would send help! I was saved! I lowered my arms finally — they didn't even feel tired or achy, I was drunk by then with exhaustion. Suddenly it occurred to me to look and see which Tehillim I had said a while ago, the one that got me to pray after all those years. I looked down. The book was still open: it was chapter ten, verse ten — 10:10. The thought popped into my head that the whole time I was praying with my arms reaching up, I'd had one hand at ten o'clock and one at two. On a watch dial that would make 10:10. Automatically I looked at my own watch. It was exactly 10:10.

Williams leaned back in his chair and rolled his eyes. "That's it? That's the big deal? That's the secret of 10:10?"

he said loudly. "You shook up an entire advertising industry just to boast about the time you were rescued?" Anger
came over his face. "I had to come all the way from New
York to hear about an ego trip? You just wanted the whole
world to see what time it was when a helicopter came!"

Leibel lifted his hand, looking pained. "No, it wasn't a
personal advertisement. You're quite wrong. Nor was it
any kind of egotistical tribute to my rescue. That's not it
at all. You have no idea what this is all about." Williams
began to look puzzled instead of enraged. Leibel continued,
encouraged, "If you've come so far to hear my story, please
calm down and let me tell it." Williams now looked intrigued. He nodded silently, and Leibel took up his tale.

———————————

When the rescue team arrived, about an hour later, I
babbled at them to forget about me and look for Milo.
Then I had to explain who Milo was, and also convince
them I wasn't hallucinating.

While they were getting me onto the stretcher I heard
someone shout, "He's over here!" Then I heard sounds of
rocks being moved. One of the team came over and told
me that Milo had been buried. By that time I was fading
fast: I remember thinking fuzzily, "If he's already buried,
why dig him up?"

Later on I understood that Milo got banged around a
lot worse than I did. The good news was that his injuries
turned out not to be life-threatening, or irreversible. The
medics found he only had a cracked skull, some broken
ribs, and a concussion.

But I — well, it took four men to get that rock off me. The helicopter took Milo to the hospital, still unconscious, then it came back for me. We were both put in Bakersfield General Hospital, and that's where they told me that all the bones below my knee were crushed.

They brought Milo around pretty soon, and after a few days he was on the mend. We were both in the hospital, although in different wings, for about a month. I finally got around to asking the medics how they found us so quickly, and they told me that the taxi driver who had dropped us off thought of us when he heard about a tremor near Middle Palisades and had alerted the rescue services. Easy enough: the taxi driver remembered us. But in my opinion that only happened because I remembered God.

My wife Lena flew in from Scarsdale. I got a giddy, warm feeling when I saw her and the kids — I'd been feeling for a while like I might not ever see them again. Curtis was one of the first ones to call, and I was mighty relieved that he didn't say, "I told you so." He just stuck to business, mainly briefing me on how the ad agency would function until I could come back. That day we skirted the issue of how much I'd be up to when I did come back.

It was pretty boring in hospital. One day, though, I had an unusual visitor, with a long black beard and a black hat. I hadn't seen anyone wearing a hat for years and years. He looked a lot like one of the Rabbis I remembered from my years in the yeshivah.

I didn't recognize him, but he came right over, put out his hand, and said, "Shalom aleichem. I'm Baruch Steinberg,

Milo's uncle. I flew in to visit Milo, and I thought I'd drop in on you too and see how you're feeling."

We talked for a while, and when I asked him what he did for a living, he said he sold diamonds and had his own shul in his basement. I thought that sounded really weird, "selling diamonds and running a shul." A shul doesn't make money! I'd have to ask him about that later, I thought. I never did, but nowadays I understand — he meant a living for his soul.

Anyway, I remembered Milo mentioning this uncle to me once. He'd said Uncle Baruch was the one most like his grandmother among the family. I told Baruch a bit about my past, how I went to yeshivah, and then I told him how I'd read from Milo's grandmother's Tehillim, and I thought those prayers had saved me.

There was an awkward silence in the room. Baruch seemed choked up for a moment. Then he caught himself and tremblingly told me how Milo's grandmother was a holy person, and maybe her merit had something to do with me being saved. He also told me that really shook me: how for generations Tehillim had kept Jews going even when their situation was bleak.

Suddenly Baruch's eyes lit up, "Did you *bentsch gomel?*"

My forehead wrinkled. "That sounds familiar, but I can't remember what it means."

"Oh, it's a special blessing that's said after you make it alive through a dangerous situation. You really should say it in front of ten men. Here, I brought my Siddur, let me show it to you." He handed me his Siddur, and when I touched it, it seemed to give off the same electrical impulses that the old Tehillim had. He showed me the *berachah*, and I don't know why, but I found myself asking him a question: "How come God's name is abbreviated in all the *berachos*?" (In a Siddur God's name isn't written out in full, it appears as an abbreviation, two letter *yuds* one after the other.) He didn't know the answer to that, but we talked for a while, and afterwards he said that he'd come back tomorrow, but I could keep his Siddur for the meantime.

Once he left, the first thing I wanted to do was take a look at the Siddur. I figured that I might as well start from the beginning, and turned to the first page. It showed the *aleph-beis* — the Hebrew alphabet — and below each letter was its *gematria*. Hebrew letters have a numerical value: for example, *aleph*, the first letter, is one, *beis*, the second letter, is two, and so on. When I came to the tenth letter, *yud*, I felt as if the floodgates of my heart had just opened. Two *yuds* — the abbreviation for God's name — is 10-10. The time I was saved, the verse in Tehillim I was reading, the position of my arms when the helicopter came, and now the numerical value of the letters of God's name — all of them 10:10! My heart started doing somersaults. I knew I was on to something. I had to keep that promise I made on the mountain.

About a month later I was discharged from the hospital and was able to go back to New York. It was — well, a little hard — to get used to a wheelchair. And I had to go regularly to a hospital in Manhattan for treatments.

What with recovering from injuries, and physiotherapy, and learning wheelchair tactics, and trying to run the agency, the days were very full. In particular, somehow or other I just didn't have much contact with Milo. A few times I called him to see how he was doing, but every time he was gruff with me and cut me off short. I took it in my stride — I mean, he had some serious injuries, and I knew from my own experience that it must be hard for him.

Then one day I ran into him in the hospital. He was in the waiting room waiting for some test results. I was happy to see him, and wheeled myself over to him. "Milo, how are you feeling?" I asked.

He just looked up at me. He didn't seem too happy. I didn't know how to get a conversation going. What had he found out? Obviously it must have been something shattering.

In the end I just sat there and waited for him to speak. Finally he mumbled, "They said there might be permanent damage to my shoulder."

"Oh," I said tentatively. "I'm sorry."

"Do you realize what that means?" he shot back hotly. "I might not be able to tee off properly ever again."

"Tee off?" I asked incredulously. "As in golf?"

"That's right, golf. They told me there's a chance that I might not be able to play pain-free ever again."

At this point I couldn't stay silent. "Milo! We were both saved from a disaster! Don't you realize we could easily have both been killed? We have to be grateful to the Almighty for saving us."

Milo just shrugged his shoulders. "What good is being saved without golf?"

I didn't stay long after that. I made a couple of fumbling attempts at conversation, but it wasn't working. I haven't seen Milo much since then. He sank into a sort of permanent depression, and it was hard to talk to him at all, much less talk about what I really wanted to say.

A couple of months later, I was able to attend the annual watchmakers' convention in Geneva. All of my big accounts were there, as well as some manufacturers I hadn't landed yet. I was taken aback when I quickly became the celebrity of the convention. Come to think of it, I never asked how they knew; I guess they must have read about the accident in the newspapers. However it happened, everyone wanted to hear my story. But the biggest surprise came when Steve Michaels, (he was president of one of the big companies) shook my hand and said, "A few of us want to take you out for a bite after the evening program."

I thought, "That's a switch. They're wining and dining me for a change." That evening Michaels took me to one of the most expensive restaurants in Geneva — the very same one I had treated him to on other occasions.

When I rolled my chair into the private banquet room, my eyes widened in shock. I couldn't believe how many people were there. As I scanned the room I recognized most of the faces: almost all of my "accounts" were there, as well as a few belonging to my competitors.

After the meal they asked me to get up and speak. They wanted to know just what happened to me in California. I grabbed my crutches and, with an effort, stood at the front of the room. There was total silence, almost nerve-wracking, for a few moments while I gathered my thoughts.

I hadn't prepared anything, so I just spoke from my heart. It was the first time I'd ever given a plain descriptive account of something, without hype, and I put all the emotion I had into it. I just wanted them to picture what I'd gone through.

My voice cracked a few times, and I noticed some of the crowd rubbing their eyes. I told about the promise I made on the mountain, how I was saved at 10:10, and then my discovery that God's name is represented with *yud yud*. Many of these big businessmen were Jewish, so I wasn't saying anything that was so very foreign to them.

I wound up by saying, "For the first time in over twenty years, I prayed with everything I had, and I was answered. So I'm quite sure that I must keep the promise I made on the mountain.

"I have a favor to ask of you, to help me keep my promise to God. I want you all, in every ad from now on, to put the hands of the watch you display at the time 10:10.

"I'm not asking this only for myself. It's for you too. I know you men very well, and I know that you do your business with honesty and integrity. But the competition can get cutthroat. Sometimes we all feel the need to play a few tricks. If you grant my request, from now every ad will be a reminder: if you want to play shenanigans, just look at the hands of your watches. They'll help you remember that one day you'll have to answer to the One above. The hands of the watch will be at 10:10, *yud-yud*,

God's own name. God is watching us.

"In the hospital I read a Psalm where God is referred to as *Shomer Yisrael*, the watchman of Israel. When you look at the watch-hands, remember who is watching you. Before you do anything slippery, think how you'll explain it some day to God."

I couldn't believe I had the nerve to ask such a thing. But I guess they all felt some sympathy with what I said; certainly, afterwards when they shook my hand and told me how much they enjoyed my speech, they told me they'd go along with it. I couldn't have been more surprised — or more pleased.

The next day at the convention, I spoke to some other manufacturers who hadn't been at the restaurant. I gave them a brief version of what I'd said the evening before, and used my best selling skills to ask them to put their watches too at 10:10. Almost every one of them agreed. A few were uncertain, but, as I found out later, Michaels talked them into it. (Talk about amazing things!) He used the tactic of pointing out to them that it wouldn't cost anything, and that nobody would notice the change. By the end of the convention, every single manufacturer had agreed. When the holiday-season watch ads appeared a few months later, all the hands were at 10:10, and it's been that way ever since.

After looking at the ad catalogues, I made up my mind to go and see Milo one last time. I had to show him all the watches set to that one time, and tell him why they were. Also, I had never gotten around to returning his Tehillim.

By this time Milo was deep into his depression. But when I showed him the watch ads he seemed to come alive. Then I found out why: he thought that 10:10 was an insider ego-trip celebrating our rescue. When I told him what it really meant, and what I'd done at the convention, his face hardened. From that moment he didn't want to hear another word, especially not anything about God. Eventually I gave up, and moved to my second errand. I reached in my attaché case and put his grandmother's old Tehillim on the table. "At least take this back," I said softly, "and use it sometimes to pray."

Milo looked up at me with a look — I can only describe it as shocked. "How could I ever pray again to a God that ruined my golf game?" he asked. I was stunned, unable to answer a word, so Milo went on. "It's your thing; you keep the Tehillim."

I never found a way past his barriers, or whatever it was; and then I left America, you know, and I haven't spoken to him since. I kept the Tehillim, though, and I still read from it almost every day.

I guess that Michaels was really taken up with my idea. A few years later, when he was dabbling in some other business affairs, he even acquired an interest in a radio station in New York whose frequency was 1010, and he's been pushing those numbers on the air ever since.

But we kept the message itself an industry secret, just among ourselves. You can see now why I was so reluctant to tell you the whole story.

———————————

Leibel looked up at Williams' astonished face. His guest was just recovering himself. Finally Williams asked, "Did it work?"

Leibel grinned. "Look at the corporate scandals going on today. Inflated earnings, debt concealed to cheat investors, embezzling, and lying, all have become standard practices. You've seen what happened to Enron and World-Com. Did you notice that none of the watch manufactures are ever involved in this monkey business?

"Have you ever heard of anyone complaining about a watch? These manufacturers probably have the highest level of owner satisfaction in the world." Leibel's eyes were flashing as he spoke passionately. "No matter what brand you buy or how much you spend, the public is always satisfied. Do you realize that no major watch company has gone belly-up in the past fifty years? All that is because of 10:10. The manufacturers always knew God was watching and they'd better keep in line. The truth stared them in the face every time they looked at their very own ads."

"But recently a few companies aren't putting 10:10 on their watches. What happened?"

"They're being run by a new generation of executives. The young ones have been taught about the 10:10 idea — I made sure of that — but some of them have fallen victim to the current corporate environment. They've made up their minds that they'll cheat if they need to, and they don't want anything in their ads that implies God is watching them."

Williams cleared his throat. "Well, ok, but I once had a digital watch, and it barely lasted two weeks before—"

"Digital?" cut in Leibel. "Oh please, most of them are cheap junk. Anyway, I have little influence over those companies. The LCD display didn't come in until the 70s, when I was starting to slow down, so I never got many accounts from that sector. Perhaps you didn't notice that none of those are ever advertised with the time 10:10. No; it's only the precision instruments that show that sign, and they are still made with integrity."

Williams leaned forward and put his hand on his forehead as if he had a sudden pain. For a while he shook his head back and forth silently. Then he looked up with a face full of bewilderment and said only, "Why? Why the big secret?"

Leibel smiled quizzically. "How did you expect me to publicize it? Put a notice in fine print in the ads? This was something only for the company bosses. It just made sense to keep the whole matter under wraps."

Williams sat back in his chair and stared at the clock over Larry's desk, silently digesting all he had heard. He watched the second hand go around in its perfect intervals. "I knew all along I was on to a story," he thought, "but I never realized what effects a simple ad could have." Aloud he said, "Mr. Gaines, I appreciate your letting me in on this secret. Do I have your permission to publicize everything you've just told me?" Now he looked straight at Leibel. Although he had regained some color, and a weight seemed to have been removed from his shoulders, he had a serious expression on his face.

"I don't have a problem with it, except..."

"Except for what?"

"The message of 10:10 is really for the Jewish people. They're the ones who are commanded to think about God all the time. I don't think you're going to reach the Jewish people through your website. If you could, I'd give you permission. If the Jewish people took this message to heart, and did everything knowing that God is watching their every move, it could help bring the Messiah."

"But my website is the ideal way! We have over a million hits a month."

"Yes... but still, I'd like first to publicize it just to the Jewish people, before you put it on your website."

Williams looked at the desk, frustrated. How was he supposed to do that? Suddenly he exclaimed, "Wait! I have an idea. That author I quoted for the Colin Powell story — what was his name... Roth. Let's contact him! I'll give him a copy of this tape, and he can release the story of 10:10 to a Jewish publisher. I'll wait until then before I put anything on my website. How about it?" He suddenly grinned. "Maybe the guy will even call his next book after this story."

Leibel smiled from ear to ear. "Great idea!"

Taking Stock

Meir plopped himself down by the kitchen table, poured himself a cup of Cristal Cola, and opened the latest *Jewish Commentator*. He groaned; his back was aching from cleaning the oven for Pesach. Suddenly he giggled. His wife Devorah was at the sink, cleaning a chicken, and asked, "What's so funny?"

"The back cover of this supposedly Torah-true magazine has a full-color ad, with a beautiful swimming pool, for Pesach in Beverly Hills. Is that the best way of celebrating leaving Egypt? By going to Beverly Hills?"

Devorah said, her back bent over the sink, "I know it sounds crazy, but Pesach is so expensive in America, some people save up and combine it with a vacation." He was about to retort, "It's not so cheap here either," but before he could say it the phone rang. Devorah quickly picked it up. While she was talking, he noticed for the first time how red her hands looked from all the scrubbing. He lifted his gaze from her hands to her face, and was immediately worried. Devorah's face had turned a bit pale, and now he noticed the frustration in her voice. He heard her say, *"Kamah?... Mah mispar ha-check? ... matai chazar?"*

Except for the word *selichah,* which she used repeatedly, he couldn't understand much of the conversation — Devorah's Hebrew was a lot better than his. But Meir caught enough that his heart sank to his stomach. "Oh no. Not another one of those calls," he thought as he put his head in his hands and stared at the floor.

Devorah hung up the phone and confirmed it: "Another check bounced." This time the apprehension in her voice was obvious. Meir tensed even more — if even Devorah didn't know what to do this time....

Meir didn't look up. He couldn't. "How much?" he groaned.

"Four hundred and eighty shekels, from the *makolet*." She looked down at him with her hands dangling and asked limply, "How're we going to pay it off?"

Meir stammered, "Well, I suppose we could...."

Forceful now, Devorah interrupted, "That's number eight. Two more and we're *mugbal*."

Meir froze. He hated hearing that word. If you bounced ten checks in six months, under Israeli law your account got frozen. No more writing checks on that account for a whole year. And meanwhile everyone expects you to hand them a series of post-dated checks to pay for everything....

Meir took a deep breath and looked up at Devorah. He saw the fear in her face and looked down again. It had come into his head to tell her about a new *gemach* that just opened, but when she mentioned the dreaded word *mugbal* he knew that yet another loan wasn't going to solve this. His head started racing; words he'd been holding back for a long time came rushing out. "I can't take much more of this."

Devorah froze. Then she said uncertainly, "More of what?"

"Bounced checks, running to one *gemach* to pay off the other, missing mortgage payments," Meir said. The bitterness was clear in his voice.

Devorah stammered, "Everyone else in Aretz lives the same way."

"Maybe everyone else is used to it. I'm not. I need to have some way to live! I want to be able to pay my bills. I'm not used to being dirt poor, with nothing even to pay for the food I eat. Do you know what it's doing to me, going on like this? And now we're going to end up *mugbal!*

"The other day a kid in my shiur was showing off the inside of his wallet. It was full of hundred-dollar bills! His father must have given them to him. He told me that he's flying home to Boro Park for Pesach. First class, yet! And I — not only can't I afford plane fare, I can't even pay my grocery bill!"

Devorah realized by now that she'd been wrong to mention "the *m* word," but it was too late. Now what to do? Meir had always been so strong; she didn't know how to handle this new face of his. Well, at least now she knew how he was feeling. She sat down next to her husband at the kitchen table and said gently, "Eretz Yisrael is bought with suffering." She was hoping that line would work. It usually did.

This time it only seemed to get him more aroused. "How much suffering am I supposed to put up with?" he yelled. Devorah jumped. "We didn't have these problems in America. There you even get to spend Pesach in Beverly Hills!"

He stood still for a few moments, looking down at the table. Devorah sat silent, wondering how she'd missed how much Meir was hurting. She didn't know what to say to him any more.

"Should I tell her now?" thought Meir. In that instant he made up his mind. He looked up at his wife and said slowly, "I've been thinking. Maybe it's time I looked into things over there."

Devorah gasped, less at Meir's words than at his flat tone of despair. Was he serious? She opened her eyes wide and said in shock, "What do you mean?"

"My uncle sent me a letter a few days ago. He's got hold of a possible entry-level position in a stock brokerage on Wall Street."

Devorah's head was spinning. Along with all the pressures of getting ready for Pesach, this was too much. After a few deep breaths she got hold of herself a bit and stammered, "You mean we should move? Leave Yerushalayim? ... Live in New York?"

Meir said firmly, "I'm thinking about it."

Devorah took another deep breath. A dozen possible issues came rushing into her head, and she rattled them off as they came. "Danny can't read English... I have no friends there... the kids are doing well in school here... we'll all need new wardrobes... I'll need a fancy *shaitel* just to go to the supermarket...."

Meir interrupted her. "I know all that, but I can't take much more of living like this." He looked at his watch. "Oh my! I'd better leave now if I want to make my *chavrusa* on time. Look, we'll talk more later." He grabbed his worn-out blue sports coat from the chair by the dining-room table, stuck his hat on, and ran out the door. Devorah sat there at the table in shock for a few moments, then picked up the phone.

Whenever he was learning with Gavriel, Meir would stop worrying. They usually learned night *seder*, but for the weeks leading up to Pesach they had both registered for vacation learning in a *Kollel bein hazmanim*.

About an hour into the *seder* Meir got up to use the bathroom. As he washed his hands he was surprised to find Gavriel standing in the hall outside the doors of the Beis Midrash, obviously waiting for him. At his questioning look, Gavriel said, a bit uneasily, "Do you need a loan to tide you over this Pesach?"

Meir smiled and shook his head. "I think I can arrange something with a *gemach*. Thanks for asking."

Gavriel added softly, "Your wife called me just before I left. She sounded worried. Are you really serious about this New York thing?"

Meir stopped for a second and tugged at his beard. "I'm looking into it."

"She's really concerned, Meir. Look, you own your apartment in Yerushalayim. Your kids are doing well in school. We all have financial pressures, but you're a Rebbe at…"

Meir's bitter smirk at the word "Rebbe" stopped Gavriel in mid-sentence. "Problems at the *yeshivah ketanah*?"

Meir was silent for a moment. Gavriel didn't say anything. Finally Meir blurted out, "I didn't tell Devorah the whole story of what happened the other day."

"About what?"

"A kid in my shiur was showing off his wallet, full of hundred-dollar bills, if you can believe that. This kid has been a troublemaker all year, always putting down the other kids, never paying attention in class, acting up a lot. I think the only reason they let him in was to be on his father's good side. Anyway, I told him he should really try to behave, and that it's hard to teach with all his interruptions. He told me back, 'I don't have to listen to you. My father makes more money in a week than you do in a year.'"

Gavriel looked at Meir and said sympathetically, "So one kid put you off...."

"It's not just one kid. I realize the yeshivah is for English-speaking kids who need *chizuk*, but how much do I have to put up with? As soon as they go back to America, everything I've taught them goes out the window. I heard that some of them aren't even *frum* any more today. So what good did I do them? Did I accomplish anything?

"I spend hours every day preparing my *shiur*. Do you think these guys remember a word of it? At night, instead of reviewing it, they sneak out to the movies or they hang out on Yaffo Street."

"You never know the impact you're making...."

"Look, Gavriel, I was told that a Rebbe is like a sculptor. He chips away the bad parts until in the end he leaves a work of art. But for Heaven's sake! Even Gutzon Borglum, when he carved Mount Rushmore, saw more progress than I'm seeing! I get flack from the parents and appreciation from no one. I could even deal with the overdrafts and the bounced checks at the grocery store if at least I felt I was making an impact on someone. But I don't see that happening. So if I'm not doing anything useful with this hand-to-mouth life I'm living, I have to get a real job and make a real living. The rest is just logic: since I don't speak Hebrew very well, my only option is to look for a job in America."

For once Gavriel was silent. He could find no answer to this *kushya.*

The next few days found Meir making several long-distance calls to the States. It seemed to his wife that he was spending more time on the phone than he did preparing what he'd say at the *seder.* Devorah mentioned this to him quietly, but he didn't seem to pay any attention. She was starting to feel that she was living with a man she'd never seen before.

Soon Meir found a cheap plane ticket to New York, on a flight after Pesach. Fortunately he was able to pay for it with twenty-four post-dated checks. "Hopefully," he thought, "these checks will clear. No, I'm going to see to it that they do clear. I'm going to change things!"

Once he had picked up the ticket, it began to dawn on him that the move might really happen. The effect was unexpected. Jerusalem always looked gray in the early Nisan rain; now it seemed grayer than ever. As he rode the bus home he found himself feeling sad, instead of rejoicing over the coming Yom Tov. "This could be my last Pesach in Yerushalayim," he thought morosely. "Am I doing the right thing?" He knocked the thoughts around his head during the whole bus ride, and was surprised when he found himself home so quickly. He faked a smile as he came through the door. Devorah did the same when he showed her the ticket.

Pesach that year was a subdued affair. The Seder lacked Meir's usual insights, and more importantly, his enthusiasm. His three children were still young, however, and he somehow managed to keep them interested at the table. "They should be able to adjust to America fine," he thought to himself.

In the middle of turning the house back to chametz Devorah asked, "Before you leave, don't you think you should get a *berachah* from R. Nissan?"

The household had gotten a bit tense ever since Meir began talking about his trip. Devorah had tried her best to point out the benefits of living in Eretz HaKodesh, but Meir, while he took it all in, felt he had no choice. This suggestion, however, he thought, was a good one. Until now he hadn't asked a Rav if he was doing the right thing, so a visit to R. Nissan Garowitz was in order.

From the ground-floor apartment in Givat Shaul it was a single bus ride to R. Nissan's home in Beis Yisrael. Since Pesach fell at the end of March that year, some light rain had left the Yerushalayim sidewalks damp. Meir hugged his worn black coat tight as he waited for the bus. He heard his teeth chattering — he wasn't sure if it was only from the cold wind. Now that Pesach was over and the trip more or less planned, it again dawned on him what he was planning. Thoughts flew around his head like *charoses* in the blender. "Do I really want to leave Eretz Yisrael? Do I want to raise my children in America? Maybe I could find a better-paying job here in Jerusalem. But what could I do? I don't speak Hebrew too well. What about the tax breaks I'd lose once I leave my teaching post?" His thoughts were interrupted when he suddenly saw a bus with its doors swinging open.

He found a seat toward the back and smiled at the cross-section of Jews getting on. With a lurch the bus pulled forward, and Meir stared aimlessly out the window. "At least," he thought, "here I'm with my people. America is the land of the goyim. There are nice Jewish communities there, sure, but it's not our place. Jews belong in Israel. But do I have a choice? How could I stay in teaching? Am I even accomplishing anything?"

Before he knew it the bus was in the Geulah district. Meir joined the line of people getting off on Malchei Yisrael Street.

Near R. Nissan's house Meir paused for a moment, gazing at an old shul. The lights reflecting off the moist Jerusalem stone made him stop and think. His forehead wrinkled. "This building will no doubt stay a shul even after the Mashiach comes. In New York most of the shuls in the South Bronx are now churches and mosques. And in Europe, how many shuls survived the war? How much longer will it be until the same thing happens in Monsey and Boro Park?" He felt a pain in the back of his throat. "So how could I move my family to America?"

As Meir looked down for a moment, a yellow glare from the road caught his eye. It was the reflection of a neon sign over the local bank. His account was in the Givat Shaul branch of the same bank. The sight suddenly reminded him of the dreaded word *mugbal* that hovered over his account. From there he went on to remember the incident with the hundred-dollar bills. His mood was shattered; he increased his pace toward R. Nissan's home.

He quickly found the apartment and knocked on the door. A few moments later he was looking at R. Nissan's smiling face. Meir followed the Rav into the small dining room area that doubled as his study.

Meir sat down and, after a few short courtesies, poured out everything that had been on his mind for the last few weeks: the financial hardships, the lack of satisfaction in his job, and his vague plans for the future. The words flowed like a burst water pipe. All the while R. Nissan sat in his chair, offering occasional comments, but mostly just listening.

Finally, after Meir had stopped, R. Nissan said, "I'm going to tell you two stories.

"The first one I heard many years ago at a Torah U-Mesorah convention. I never checked if it was true, but I think I should tell it over anyway. — In the Polish Navy, after much cajoling, the Rabbanim managed to arrange for a kosher kitchen. Some Jews who ate there soon complained that some not-so-religious Jewish soldiers were going for seconds to the treifeh kitchen!

"'We're not letting those fakers in,' the sailors said. 'Let them go and eat treifeh if they want it.' When the Chafetz Chaim heard about it, he demanded that they be let in. 'One more *kazayis kosher*,' he said, 'is one less *kazayis treifeh*.' In teaching it's the same thing. You teach a child a piece of Torah, a *vort*, a bit of Gemara — something may settle in, you don't ever know. But you know you handed him one more bit of Torah to offset all the *treifeh* the rest of the world will give him."

Meir sat frozen with his mouth open. He'd never considered things that way.

"Here is the other story that comes to my mind. Yaakov was a poor shoemaker who barely was able to support his large family. The added expense of giving his eldest daughter a dowry made the situation desperate. In search for a way out, he went to visit his Rebbe. He had to wait in the courtyard for many hours, but finally, when he was exhausted and cold, Nissan had his turn for an audience. Just as the *shamash* opened the door to let him in, he heard the Rebbe making a slow, careful *berachah* on a cup of tea, finishing '...*shehakol nihyah bidevaro.*' Yaakov thought for a moment, 'Everything exists by His word. Everything comes from Hashem. He controls all events, all actions, all situations in this world. Everything that happens, every person you meet, is arranged, a part of the gigantic master plan. *Shehakol nihyah bidevaro.*'

"After Yaakov heard those three words from his Rebbe's mouth, he didn't bother going in. He had the inspiration he had come for. Hashem will provide everything: financially, spiritually, and emotionally.

"Meir, you just have to learn to trust Him, *shehakol nihyah bidevaro*, by Whose word all things exist. Both here and in America, *parnassah* comes from above. All that is left for me to do is to give you a *berachah* to have a safe and successful trip."

Meir had trouble sleeping that night, especially since he had to be at the airport at six in the morning. After 9/11 there were a lot of added security measures. But anyway his mind wouldn't let him sleep — the thoughts were flying even faster than they had on the bus to R. Nissan's house. What exactly did the Rav mean by that second story?

He found no answers in the morning. After the trip to Ben Gurion Airport, check-in, and the long search procedure, by the time he finally got on the plane he was so exhausted that he slept most of the flight. Ten hours later, when the plane landed at JFK, he still felt exhausted. Somehow he managed to track down his luggage, and was delighted when he saw, as planned, his brother-in-law waiting for him. "It was really nice of him to meet me at the airport," thought Meir. "At least I save money on the carfare."

The next day the ride on the Monsey bus was grueling. He wondered out loud how anyone could make this trip day in and day out. He cringed for a moment when he realized that soon he might be doing the same.

After most of the passengers got off at 47th and 5th Ave., Meir stayed on the bus all the way to the Wall Street area. He found Global International easily enough, then made it through the maze of offices, until he finally arrived at the personnel department for his interview.

While sitting in the waiting area, he was shocked when he heard a voice saying, "Rabbi Gonshack? Is that you?" That didn't sound like the secretary. In fact the voice sounded familiar. He looked up from his sefer, but couldn't recognize the face of the young man in front of him. There was a vaguely familiar look, but that weird haircut and the earring certainly didn't ring a bell. The ultra-modern suit was also a bit out of place.

Sensing the Rabbi's confusion, the young man said, "Gladstone. You knew me as Chaim. Now it's Kevin. How're ya doing, Rabbi?"

Meir sat speechless for a few seconds. This was Chaim Gladstone? One of his former *talmidim?* "I guess I shouldn't act surprised," he thought. He stood up and extended his hand, stammering, "Chaim... I mean Kevin! How have you been?"

Kevin shook Meir's hand and said in a shaky voice, "I'm fine, Rabbi. How are you?" Was that apprehension in Kevin's voice?

Meir answered, *"Baruch Hashem,* I'm fine. Do you work here?"

"I'm in the personnel department. What brings you here? You collecting for the yeshivah?"

Meir said softly, "Actually, I'm looking for an entry-level position as a broker."

Instantly Kevin's face convulsed as he snickered and rolled his eyes, while Meir stood there with a blank expression on his face. Then Chaim — Kevin — recovered himself and said with a strange smile, "Rabbi, I hope you don't mind me saying so, but I think you'll have a hard time making it here."

Meir took a half step back. "Why?" he asked, bewildered. What would make Kevin say a thing like that?

"Why? I'll tell you why." Kevin's face began to flush. "You heard about Enron's collapse. Hidden debts, faked profits, inflated stocks. It's usually not so bad, but stuff like that, a little or a lot like it, happens on Wall Street all the time. For too many people around here it's not about earning money, it's about manipulating money. Are you sure you want to be a part of a world that has people like that in it?"

Meir stood silent, thinking hard, while Kevin went on. "I picked a more honest firm to work for — a lot more honest than most. But every day, even in this firm, you're put to the test. It's hard be one hundred percent straight all the time. Just a little bit of exaggerating, or withholding a certain piece of information, can make the difference in netting you a huge commission. Sometimes I was tempted play a few tricks. It was hard, really hard to say no. You can't imagine what the temptation is like. Especially when you begin to see that your ultimate success depends on giving in sometimes."

Meir blinked. That last bit had to be an exaggeration. "Are you telling me everyone on Wall Street steals?" he asked.

Kevin sighed. "No... I do know some honest people. It's just that, if you want a promotion, you have to bring in big bucks. And to do that, so often it seems that you have to play a few tricks. You know why I'm stuck in the personnel department? I couldn't pull in big sums as frequently as some others, so they reassigned me here."

"Why couldn't you 'play the game'?" Meir asked curiously.

"I don't really know," answered Kevin, looking more troubled every moment. "There were just things that I couldn't make myself do. Not stealing, not exactly cheating, but — I just couldn't." He paused, then pulled the words up from deep within him. "You know, sometimes I remember how you mentioned about how we're gonna have to answer upstairs for whatever we do down here. It's hard to be — well, let's say 'clever' — when you know you'll have to answer for it. I sometimes feel that a few other guys I know have an advantage over me. They don't have this little voice in their heads like I do, telling me the truth."

"Little voice?"

"Yeah. And come to think of it, sometimes that little voice sounds kinda like you."

Meir stood there speechless. Strange, how suddenly he felt that a burden had fallen off his shoulders. A warm feeling filled his heart.

Abruptly he turned back to the secretary. "I'm sorry, I won't be able to keep my appointment."

"Yes sir. Do you want to reschedule?"

"No thank you. I plan on being on the next flight to Jerusalem."

Now he turned to Kevin, and for the first time in weeks squared his sagging shoulders. "It was worth coming from Israel just to hear you tell me these things," he told Kevin with a smile.

For his part, Kevin could see a new confidence flowing into his old Rebbe. He thought he understood what was happening. It was enough to smile back.

On his way out Meir stopped to take a drink from the water cooler. Loud enough for Kevin to hear, he said with perhaps the best *kavanah* he'd had for some time, "...*sheha-*

kol nihyah bidevaro!" As he took a sip Kevin instinctively answered, "Amen."

Then Kevin watched as a transformed Rabbi Gonshack approached him and vigorously shook his hand in farewell. As he walked away Kevin noticed that the Rabbi seemed to have a lively step. And how odd, he was muttering something over and over, something barely audible. Suddenly Kevin made it out. For some reason his old teacher was saying over and over again, *"Shehakol nihyah bidevaro... shehakol nihyah bidevaro... shehakol nihyah bidevaro...."*

The Plane Truth

Although he wasn't very religious, Shmuel Katz liked Chol HaMoed Sukkos. It was good for business. The impression he had was that the only time decent crowds came to his Aviation Museum was during Pesach and Sukkos.

Soon after the museum opened that day, Katz walked into the box office. It was so small that it barely held two people. Through the glass windows he could see, for a change, people waiting on line to get in. He said to Blumeh, his ticket-taker, "It looks like we'll have plenty of people today."

Blumeh smiled behind her curly brown hair. "It must be the weather. At least now it's not so hot. I don't blame them for not coming during the summer. I can't take the summers in Be'er Sheva either."

Katz again looked at the line. He lifted his chin and smiled, and for an instant had a feeling of pride. It was his idea to show the "special planes" only during the holiday season. He had started this museum after serving in the Israeli Air Force — eight years it had been in all, including the Sinai War in 1956. Could it really be six years already since then?

After leaving the Service he had realized people might be interested in seeing fighter planes of the Israeli Air Force. He'd started his museum with some decommissioned planes that had been used during the war. Nowadays there were also a few older planes, but he was an Air

Force man at heart: his private opinion was that the museum could do as well without the "oldies." It was only at the urging of the museum's historian, Azriel Hecker, that he'd persuaded the museum's financial board to find funds for them.

Katz decided to wander around the grounds. A good day, all right: it wasn't often there were so many people. In anticipation of Chol HaMoed crowds he had stationed guides all around who would explain, in Hebrew or English, the significance of each one of the museum's aircraft. As he passed by one of the oldest models, the Boeing Condor, he stopped suddenly and stared in shock. He rarely paid attention to the "oldies," and hadn't even glanced at this one in a long time. It was in awful shape. Some of the chassis' metal plates were barely hanging on. He could see rust holes in the roof. The paint was peeling off of the fuselage and wings.

"Just my luck," he thought. "The one day the crowds are here!"

As he stood off to the side, he heard Hecker reciting to a group, "This Boeing Condor is 38 feet long and has a wingspan of 55 feet. It was built in 1937, and was used mainly as a cargo plane. This is one of the few remaining examples of the Boeing Condor left in the world. The famed American pilot Emelia Airheart was flying this model of plane when she presumably ran out of fuel and crashed into the Pacific in her attempt to be the first woman to fly solo around the world...." Katz didn't want to hear anymore. He was just hoping none of the tourists would take pictures of the peeling paint.

A few days after Sukkos, the "oldies" were once again in their hangars at the back of the grounds. Katz was in his office, just about to draw up an ad offering discounts to local residents (have to boost those dead winter months). He heard a knock on his door. "Come in," he called and looked up. Hecker had an unusual, inquisitive look on his face. "That Condor's paint is peeling."

Katz smiled wryly. "I noticed. We can't keep displaying it like that."

"I know we don't have much funds, but I'd like to do some minor refurbishing. We'll have to peel off the outer layer of paint. Just looking at it, I could tell whoever painted it didn't know what he was doing."

"Why do you say that?"

"Airplane paint doesn't usually come off wholesale like that, no matter how many years go by. They must have used the wrong base — it looks like a rush job. You know, I kinda wonder if that plane wasn't stolen somewhere along the line. 'Cause in a few spots I could see some markings under the paint, like maybe they were trying to cover them up."

Katz leaned forward. "Markings? What kind?"

"I'm not sure, you can't see much right now. But come to think of it, there may be something of historical value underneath." That was Hecker's most significant phrase: "historical value." He went on, "I'd like you to spare some of the crew so we can strip off the paint and see what's underneath. If it's nothing, we'll give her a fresh coat, and also try to repair some of the holes."

Katz smiled. "Oh, is that all? No problem, that won't

cost too much. I'll send you two guys right away."

A few days later, Katz saw Hecker in the employee's back room of the museum's small snack bar. He took a seat as Hecker was about to bite into his *bourekas*. "Find anything on the Condor?"

"Not much yet. That's why I haven't said anything yet. We did find the words — what was it? — 'PathRite travels round the world,' written below the cockpit. Isn't PathRite a supermarket chain? Sounds like this plane was a promotion of some sort for them."

Katz looked at Hecker and squinted. "Why don't you simply check the papers to see where we got it from?"

"That's the first thing I did! Like most of our planes, we got it from Amos."

Katz shook his head. Amos was the best used-vehicles dealer he'd ever seen, but like all such people, he picked up stuff everywhere. "Well, does he remember where he got it from?"

Hecker raised his eyebrows and blushed. He'd been so intent on seeing what was under the paint, he'd overlooked this obvious solution. "I'll give him a call today."

After lunch Hecker briefly stopped by the hangar. As he watched the crew slowly strip off the old paint, he wondered: Where *did* this plane come from? He went back to his office and got Amos on the phone. "No, not the fighter jet. The Boeing Condor. You know, the old plane, from around 1937. Right. Who'd you get it from? Okay, call me back when you dig it up."

Although Hecker had to prepare his address to the Rotary Club in Jerusalem later that month, he barely gave it a second thought. Over the next few days he was obsessed with the old plane, and he didn't know why. One day, just as he was examining a spot where the men were stripping paint by the propeller, he saw Blumeh ride up on her bicycle. She stood the bike on its kickstand, and, grabbing her memo pad from the basket, walked up to Hecker. "Amos called back. Here's the name of the person he got this plane from."

Hecker excitedly grabbed the paper from Blumeh. The note scribbled on it said, "Emily Steinhart, New York. Stored in hangar at Lod Airport, sold to Amos Fox Oct. 6, 1946."

Hecker raised his eyebrows. "A woman? From America yet?" He looked up at the plane, wondering, and suddenly saw an inscription coming out from under the old paint. He wasn't sure — was that the word "Kansas" there? He walked around to the other side, where he and Blumeh made out the phrase "Spirit of Kansas."

Blumeh asked, "Spirit of Kansas? Wasn't that the name of Lindbergh's plane?" She looked up at Hecker. Why did he have that shocked look on his face?

He paused, unable to speak, his eyes glued to the faded words. Blumeh started wondering if he was having an attack of some sort. Finally he whispered, "Lindbergh's plane was called 'Spirit of St. Louis.' But another famous aviator back then had a plane called 'Spirit of Kansas.' Her name was Emelia Airheart."

A few minutes later there was a loud knock on Katz's door. "Come in! and don't knock so loud."

Hecker was panting and red in the face. Sweat was dripping from his forehead. Before he could say a word Katz asked, "Where have you been, playing basketball?"

"I just — ran here — from the hangars. We're — onto something with that plane. The markings on it — they're the same as the ones on Emelia Airheart's plane. This must be a duplicate of her plane that somebody made."

Katz raised his palm. "Why do you think so?"

Hecker paused for a moment to catch his breath, then said, "The slogan *PathRite travels around the world* was painted on Emelia's plane. PathRite supermarkets sponsored all of her trips. Also, at the front of the plane we found 'Spirit of Kansas' stencilled on. That was the name of the plane she took on her final flight."

Katz paused for a second and scratched his head. "Why would anyone want to copy her airplane?" he asked.

Hecker shrugged his shoulders. "I don't know. Maybe it was some sort of tribute to her. I'm gonna write the Boeing people, give them the serial numbers of the plane — we found them all right, on the engine block and inside the cockpit — and ask them if they have any information. Also, I'll send a letter to the Emelia Airheart Birthplace and Museum." Hecker paused and grinned. "Bet you didn't know there was such a place!"

The refurbishing continued over the next two weeks. Unfortunately, nothing else significant was uncovered. Katz was now busy working on a new scheme for the museum.

Since the Cuban missile crisis had just passed, he thought a couple of military jets capable of dropping nuclear bombs might draw some crowds. The only problem was the difficulty in finding the planes; there were very few of this kind, he'd discovered, that were old enough to be retired. He was in the middle of typing yet another letter when Hecker barged in, this time not bothering to knock. He was waving a letter of his own.

Katz looked up. "You found us some fighter jets?"

Hecker was grinning and talking excitedly. "Fighter jets? I got a letter from Lyndon."

Katz squinted. "Lyndon who?"

Hecker pointed to the letter. "No, not a person. It's a town in Kansas, in the USA."

Now Katz was really confused. He sat back slightly and asked, "A guy named Lyndon in Kansas has some fighter jets for us?"

Hecker said, "No!"

"So why did you write them?"

"It's the birthplace of Emelia Airheart. They have a museum about her there, and they sent me the information about that Condor."

"Oh, that." Katz shook himself a moment. "So, what did they say?"

"That Condor is an exact duplicate of Emelia's plane." Hecker was practically twitching. "It even has the same serial numbers!"

Katz stared at Hecker for a second. "What? That's impossible."

"That's what the letter says, though. They sent me the

serial numbers of her Condor, and they're identical to the ones on our plane!"

Katz was skeptical. How could two planes, even if they were exact duplicates, have the same serial numbers? The manufacturers wouldn't do that, would they?

"I'm gonna call Boeing right now," he declared as he picked up the phone, then glanced at his watch. "Oh, too early for America. Come back here after four, I'll call then."

Hecker went around feeling anxious for the rest of the day, waiting for four o'clock to come. At exactly four he went back to the office. Katz was already reaching for the phone, and motioned for Hecker to sit down. As he dialed he said, "Its a good thing I've had some contact with the Boeing people before."

He looked down at his card file and dialed a Chicago number. "Hello? I'm calling long distance from Israel. I'd like to speak with a Mr. Jerry Brown." Seventeen seconds later he said, "Mr. Brown? My name is Shmuel Katz, and I'm calling from the Aeronautics Museum in Be'er Sheva, Israel. We have a question about a Condor 14C built in 1937. You did? Great."

Katz put his hand over the mouthpiece and said, "He got your letter, and was going to respond within the next day or so. He has all the information in front of him."

Katz listened to the phone for a bit, making noises of interest. Then he said, "Now, here is the crux of the matter. Did you ever manufacture a duplicate Condor 14C with the same serial numbers?" Hecker waited anxiously, watching Katz fiddle with a pencil. "Ah. I thought so. This is definitely strange. Thank you so much." Katz hung up the phone and noticed the anxious look on Hecker's face.

"He said, of course, that Boeing would never put an identical serial number on any of their planes, and that such a thing is unheard of. Furthermore, he has no knowledge of anyone ever making a duplicate plane."

Hecker turned red and then white. He started shaking. "What's the matter?" yelled Katz. "Azriel!" He tried unsuccessfully to hide the panic in his voice. "Are you all right?"

Suddenly Hecker leaped to his feet. "It's it!"

"It's what?"

"It's the original! That plane is the same one Emelia Airheart flew!"

Katz nearly fell off his chair. "What? Have you lost your mind? I've heard you say a dozen times that it crashed into the Pacific!"

"That's the generally accepted explanation." Hecker was calming down now, thinking hard. "But I've done a lot of reading since we started the refurbishing. Do you know that no trace of Airheart's plane has ever been found?"

Katz leaned back. "So? It crashed in the ocean. The Pacific is big enough to lose one plane."

Hecker leaned forward and placed his knuckles on the desk. "Do you know that her last radio transmission was that she was low on fuel? But she had taken enough. I can tell you the tanks were easily big enough to make the trip she'd scheduled, from Guinea to Howland Island."

Katz shook his head. What was Hecker driving at? "So, she sprung a leak or something, and ran out of gas, and the plane crashed. The ocean's so big, they couldn't find any trace of the plane. What's the big deal?"

Hecker opened his eyes wide. "I'll tell you the big deal. A plane that big — 38 feet long, with a 55-foot wing span — doesn't just disappear. Airheart had to be flying around 120 miles per hour. A plane flying that fast and crashing into the ocean would break apart into thousands of pieces. Look, planes are built a lot stronger nowadays than they were in 1937, and even they break apart when they hit the water. As for this plane, it's so flimsy I could practically peel the skin off with a can opener.

"President Roosevelt sent the entire Seventh Fleet to search the area, but they couldn't find a thing. Not a wing, not a wheel, not a seat, not a screw. They found absolutely nothing. Nothing ever washed ashore. She disappeared without a trace. And now we know why: she never crashed. That's her plane in our hangar."

Katz shook his head in disbelief. "Maybe she made an emergency landing on some remote desert island."

Hecker had the same pop-eyed expression. "So where's her plane? Twenty-five years later, and it still hasn't been found. Planes never disappear without a trace, yet that's exactly what happened in her case."

Katz sat back in his chair. Was it possible? After a few moments, however, he pounced on a thought. "Before you call the newspapers to announce your brilliant discovery, perhaps you could explain how her plane got to Be'er Sheva, of all places?"

Hecker's expression suddenly turned somber. His eyes slitted, and he stood upright from the desk. With all the excitement, this was something he hadn't considered. If it really was her plane, how did it get to Israel? He leaned back over the desk. "We must find the previous owner, assuming she's still alive. We must find Emily Steinhart." His hand shot out and grabbed the phone on Katz's desk.

"Who are you calling?" stammered Katz.

Hecker looked up and said, "Amos. He might have the information we need. — Amos? It's Hecker, from the museum. You know that Boeing Condor I asked you about a few days ago? Yeah. Could you check if the seller, Emily Steinhart, left a passport number or anything like that? Okay, look it up, and please get back to us right away."

"He said he'd look when he gets the chance. It shouldn't take long — he's already found her file."

Hecker went back to his office to read through anything about Emelia Airheart that he hadn't read yet. Katz came to his office a half hour later.

"Amos just called back. He went through the documents of sale, and they have Emily Steinhart's ID number on them."

Hecker quickly picked up the phone. "I'm calling Misrad HaP'nim" — the Ministry of the Interior, which stores Israel's population records. "Good thing my cousin works there. He'll know how to find her.

"Yossi? It's your cousin Azriel Hecker, you know, the one who works in the Air Force museum? I need you to trace an ID number for me. What I want to know is if she's still alive, and if so, what's her last known address. I know you'll have to go through a lot of files, but it's really important. Okay, here's the number: 314511231.

Thanks, I'll call tomorrow. Bye."

He looked up at Katz. "He says he'll do it when he gets a chance. I'd guess that means a day or two. I'm going back to look over how the plane is doing. I'll keep you posted."

After Hecker saw that the stripping work wasn't revealing anything interesting, he stopped off at Be'er Sheva's public library on his way home. Surprisingly, there was a book, newly sent by a contributor in America, all about Emelia Airheart. It was actually one that he hadn't yet read. He stayed up late that night reading it cover to cover.

The next day, Hecker got the call he was waiting for. He took the message and wrote it down, then took off for Katz's office. Katz knew right away why he'd come. "What did he say?"

Hecker was grinning from ear to ear. "He said he found one woman with that ID number, and according to their records she's still living in Israel. Her name is Esther Beileh Kroningsburg, and she lives in Jerusalem."

This time Katz returned the smile. "I think we have to pay Mrs. Kroningsburg a visit. Where does she live in Jerusalem?"

"Some new section called Bayit VaGan."

Katz thought it would be rude to drop in unannounced, but he discovered that Mrs. Kroningsburg had no phone, as was usually the case with ordinary citizens. So it would have to be a visit "out of the blue." The next day he picked up Hecker at seven. Hecker had dark rings under his eyes. "You didn't sleep well?"

"I stayed up late reading about Emelia, and then I

couldn't sleep. There are all sorts of crazy theories about what happened to her and her plane. One said she was captured by the Japanese and was the famous radio voice of World War II, Tokyo Rose. Another one says she stumbled through a porthole to the fourth dimension. Still another has her living with the natives on Howland Island."

The entire trip Hecker spoke about Emelia's life, and what the books said about her mysterious disappearance. Finally, around nine thirty, after a few missed turns, they found the right address. From the look they could tell that this was a new religious neighborhood. Katz, like most Israelis, kept his emergency yarmulke in the car's glove compartment, and he was fortunate to find a second one there for Hecker.

They got out of the car and cautiously climbed the steps to 31 Rechov Frankel. After Katz readjusted his yarmulke he knocked lightly on the door.

A woman answered it. At first the men couldn't tell how old she was. The *tichel* on her head offered no clue. The lines on her face betrayed some age, but she still had youthful features. Katz estimated her as between late fifties and early sixties.

"Yes?" she asked.

"We've come to speak with Mrs. Kroningsburg," Katz said quietly.

"I'm Mrs. Kroningsburg. Won't you come in?"

"Thank you."

Hecker noticed the American accent right away, although her Hebrew was quite good. The house was well kept, comfortable though small, thoroughly lived-in. After they sat down on the sofa Mrs. Kroningsburg asked, "What can I do for you?"

Katz spoke, "My name is Shmuel Katz. I'm the curator of the aviation museum in Be'er Sheva." Did she shift uncomfortably when she heard those last words? "Mr. Hecker here is the museum's historian. We've come from Be'er Sheva to speak to you about something of extreme importance."

Her eyes lit up. "All the way from Be'er Sheva? To speak to me? Whatever for?"

"We have a Boeing Condor 14C in our museum." A look of shock spread over Mrs. Kroningsburg's face. "It had been stored in a hangar in Ben Gurion Airport for a number of years before we bought it. Recently the paint started to peel off, and we uncovered some interesting markings underneath. We were wondering if you might know something about this plane."

Mrs. Kroningsburg sat back, her face pale. Then she put on a determined look and shook her head back and forth. "Me? Airplanes? I came to Israel by boat. I don't fly so much; I haven't been back to the States for years. I'm afraid you gentlemen are wasting your time. Now if you'll excuse me..."

Katz quickly interjected, "You were once known as Emily Steinhart, isn't that right?"

Mrs. Kroningsburg froze and was silent for a few moments. "Yes, that was my English name." Katz said confidently, "According to our research, you once owned the plane under discussion."

Mrs. Kroningsburg fiddled nervously with her fingers and said, "Well, as I said before, I'm afraid you gentlemen wasted your time coming all the way from Be'er Sheva. I never had an air—"

Hecker jumped in. "What do you know about Emelia Airheart?"

Mrs. Kroningsburg held still even longer this time. She looked at Hecker for a moment with a sad, piercing expression. Hecker expected that hearing the name would shake her. He hadn't anticipated the pained look.

Stumbling for words, Mrs. Kroningsburg said, "Wasn't she the one that crashed into the Pacific?"

Hecker continued, "And her plane was never found. Not a trace of it. Not a wing, not a plank, not a seat cushion. Nothing."

Mrs. Kroningsburg sat there silently.

"Perhaps you can let us know how her plane ended up in Be'er Sheva?"

Mrs. Kroningsburg held her palms. "I'm sure you gentlemen are mistaken. You must have a replica."

Hecker calmly said, "The serial numbers are the same."

Again Mrs. Kroningsburg shook her head back and forth. "I'm sorry, but I really have no information for you. You must have made a mistake. Now, if you'll excuse me, I'll have to ask you to leave, since...."

Hecker looked at Katz and lifted his eyebrows. He abruptly stood up and said, "We're so sorry to have troubled you. We believe this plane used to belong to Emelia Airheart, but we have no idea how it ended up intact and in Israel. We'll go right now to the Jerusalem Post and tell them about our find, and maybe they will...."

Suddenly Mrs. Kroningsburg jumped up. "No! Don't tell the newspapers!"

Hecker looked steadily at her, wondering. Why was she shaking? "There's something about that plane that you know and aren't telling us, isn't there?"

Mrs. Kroningsburg put on a false smile. She politely said, "Can I offer you gentlemen some tea?"

Hecker gave a passing glance to Katz, who said, "Yes, thank you."

She nimbly got up and walked into the kitchen. Hecker whispered, "What's she so afraid of if we go to the newspapers?"

Katz shrugged his shoulders. "I wish I knew."

With surprising speed Mrs. Kroningsburg returned with a small teapot and three tea cups on a tray. She put the tray down on the wooden table in front of the sofa, poured two cups, and gave each man one.

The trio sat in silence for a number of minutes, the only sounds those of the hot tea being sipped. Without warning Mrs. Kroningsburg broke the silence. Her tone was far harsher than it had been a few minutes ago. "It seems you're after a story, isn't that right, Mr. Katz?"

Katz put down his tea and lifted his palms upward. "We have to get to the bottom of the biggest mystery in aviation history: what happened to Emelia Airheart's plane, and how it came, intact, to my museum in Be'er Sheva."

She said almost in a whisper, "I'll tell you just this much: I used to own that plane. I haven't told a soul except for my husband. You must promise not to reveal a word of how it got here to anyone."

Katz didn't move. What should he say? He thought, "I wanted to announce to the world the answer to aviation's greatest riddle, and this lady wants me to keep it a secret? Still, we have to get to the bottom of this."

He looked at Hecker and softly nodded. "We promise," both said, almost in unison.

Mrs. Kroningsburg walked to the desk by the wall, opened a drawer, and took out her appointment book.

She said in a businesslike tone, "Good. Well, then, let's make a date when we can continue this meeting."

Katz nearly jumped out of his seat. "What? Why the wait? Why not right now?"

"I have to speak to my lawyer first, of course. Did you really think I would take your word for it? I want both of you to sign a binding legal agreement that not a word of what I say will leave this apartment."

Katz stared at her for a few moments. What was going on here? Was it worth it? Whatever it was, though, this lady was serious about keeping it under wraps. "Do you mean we can't ever tell anyone?" he asked, with evident anguish.

Mrs. Kroningsburg smirked drily. "I realize you have a museum to run, and you'll want to display your discovery. So, I'll make a deal with you. You keep that plane, I'll tell you all about how it ended up in Israel, and I'll provide all the documentation to prove my story is true. In exchange, you will keep the story a secret for... for...." There was a long pause.

Katz couldn't stand it. Was she teasing them? "For how

long?" he barked.

Mrs. Kroningsburg looked at him, again with the piercing but pained expression. "Until I leave this world."

Katz lifted his eyebrows. "Leave this world? That could be years!"

Mrs. Kroningsburg lifted her eyes to the ceiling briefly and answered, "Only God knows how long that will be. I'm already fifty-seven."

Katz asked, "What if we tell someone while you're still alive?"

She replied again in that business-like tone, "I'll have my lawyer put down that in that case you will owe me two million dollars."

Katz sat back heavily, stunned. Hecker asked, "Why don't you want us going to the press?"

"The reason for that is part of the story. If you do go to the press now, I'll deny everything, and convince them you two whipped up this scheme to get publicity for your museum. Do it on my terms, and you'll have the whole story and all the documentation you need."

She sat down quietly, placed her hands on her lap, and looked up brightly at Katz, then Hecker. "So, what'll it be, boys?" She sounded a lot different now from the quiet Jerusalem housewife who had invited them in. In the same mocking tone she continued, "Do you want to hear the plain truth about me and my Condor, that supposedly crashed into the Pacific? Do you want to know how we ended up here in Israel? Or will you take what you have to the press now, and see if they believe you, against me?"

What was that? "Me and my Condor"? Did she just say

"me and my Condor?" Hecker cringed. Her face did look familiar. He couldn't hold himself back. "I thought I saw your face in the books. You must be...."

"No freebies, boys." The mocking smile was now all over her face. "The story is yours in exchange for your guarantee of silence. Now, I don't have a phone, so if you'll leave me your number, I'll give you a few days to think over the deal."

She again jumped up and moved quickly to the door. "I really was planning on going swimming today, so I'll have to excuse myself. I enjoyed meeting both of you."

The second they were in the street, Hecker exclaimed, "Could it be? She's Emelia Airheart?"

Katz was silent as he approached his car and put the key in the lock. Then he ventured, "I didn't know Emelia Airheart was Jewish."

"She wasn't Jewish. At least not in all the books I've read. Now what? Do we sign and keep silent?"

Katz got in the car and opened the passenger-door lock, and Hecker got in. As he put the key in the ignition Katz ruminated, "We could release what we have to the press. With the serial numbers and all, they could prove the plane was really her plane, and we'd have a gold mine for the museum. What do we need to hear her story for?"

Hecker quickly countered, "Who's gonna believe us? We can't prove for certain that we have her actual plane. In Be'er Sheva? What would it be doing there? People will claim it's a hoax, that we faked the serial numbers just to get people to come to the museum."

The car picked up speed and made it out to Rechov

Herzl. "Why shouldn't they believe us?" Katz asked.

"I'll tell you why. The legend of Emelia Airheart is one that's going to be hard to break. I've been reading all I could about it. Nobody will buy this crazy story that she's alive and living in Israel."

Katz shrugged his shoulders. As much as he hated to admit it, Hecker was right.

When they got back to the museum they went to their offices, both in a trance. Neither could get any work done; both had the same thoughts: How could it be? Emelia Airheart is living in Bayit VaGan? She wasn't even Jewish! What if this lady is pulling a *shtick* on us? Yet she didn't ask for any money, only her privacy. Who will ever believe us if we tell the truth?

"I think we have no choice but to...." Katz looked up at Hecker, standing over his desk, and completed his sentence: "...sign the agreement and get the story. — I know, I'm thinking the same thing. I've just got to hear this lady's story."

"Right. But what's the good in hearing it? We can't tell anyone until who knows how long." Hecker got a grim expression on his face. "How many years do you think she has left?"

For answer, Katz just nodded. When the phone rang the next day, he agreed to all of Mrs. Kroningsburg's terms and set the meeting up.

Exactly two weeks later, Katz and Hecker were once again in the same seats in the apartment in Bayit VaGan.

"Please sign here, gentlemen," said Mrs. Kroningsburg

briskly, pointing to the papers on her dining-room table. Hecker went over to the table and picked up a paper, but before he could start reading his hostess announced, "I'll save you the trouble. My lawyer, who happens to be my son-in-law, drew up these documents. They say that for as long as I am alive, if any word of what I'm about to tell you leaks out for any reason, you will jointly owe me or my family two million dollars. I suggest you keep your mouths closed if you don't want to end up in court.

"In return for your silence, I grant you the right to publicize my story after my death. I have here an envelope with all the verification you will need, including my birth certificate, documents pertaining to my name changes, and proof I bought that Condor. I will have it sent to you, along with every other document I have, and a tape of today's interview, after I leave this world, whenever that may be. Any questions?"

Hecker shook his head, picked up the pen, and signed. Katz got up from his seat and did the same. Mrs. Kroningsburg took the papers and put them in a drawer in her desk. Turning, she brought in a bowl of fruit from the kitchen, and turned on a tape recorder that was waiting on the coffee table.

She picked up the microphone and paused, her eyes closing for a moment. Hecker and Katz leaned over, waiting for her to start. She gave them a quick glance and began to speak into the mike.

———————————

I guess I should start from the beginning. As you know

now, I was given the name Emily Steinhart when I was born — Esther Beileh in Yiddish. I grew up in the Lower East Side around the turn of the century. Like most Jewish families, we lived in a run-down tenement. I went to public school — there were no Jewish girls' schools back then. After school my grandmother used to teach us how to kasher chickens and how to read in Hebrew. She always seemed so calm and relaxed, despite our cramped living conditions. My mother worked in a sweatshop, hard work for long hours, but she kept going somehow and cared for us the best that she could.

I had lots of friends who were also religious, like us. But that all changed when I turned ten. It wasn't a very good year. My grandmother passed away, and that was bad enough. But soon afterwards my mother also passed away, the result of a long-standing case of tuberculosis. That's what happened to too many sweatshop workers.

I was left alone with my father. He took the loss hard, and eventually decided he wanted to start his life again, somewhere else. So, soon after the burial we packed up and moved to Berkeley, California. Even today there aren't many Jews there; back then there were hardly any. I had no choice but to fit in; after all, I was attending a public junior high school. It was slow at first, then faster and faster my father stopped doing mitzvos. A year or two after we got there, we were indistinguishable from our non-Jewish neighbors.

I felt so awkward; I didn't belong in this place. Even at home I didn't feel at home. I wanted to get away from all the pain, but what could I do? I was only eleven years old.

It all changed when I was seventeen and my father brought me to an air show near Oakland. That was the first time I saw airplanes up close. I couldn't take my eyes off of them. I was amazed that these heavy machines could be lighter than air. When it was time to leave, my father had to literally grab me and carry me off. I decided then and there that I wanted to fly one of those planes.

It took three years before I could even broach the question. In those days no one took a seventeen-year-old seriously, let alone a girl. But when I turned twenty my chance came. My father asked me what I wanted for my birthday. I was old enough now to be heard, and I was waiting for that question. I answered firmly, "Flying lessons." At first my father was taken aback — this was not the typical request of a twenty-year-old Jewish girl. In the end, though, he gave in. He made some phone calls, and found out that I had to wait until I turned twenty-one. I counted the days! On my twenty-first birthday, I got my lessons.

For my first lesson I was just a passenger. It was my first time in a plane, though, and the ride was even more exhilarating than I thought it would be. I quickly mastered the lessons, though I discovered I wasn't a naturally gifted pilot; but I wanted so much to be high in the sky. After a few months I was allowed to fly solo. I thought, "For the first time I'm in control of my destiny." I loved the feeling of freedom, flying up so close to heaven.

Naturally we couldn't afford our own airplane, but my father got me in the cockpit as much as his expenses allowed. I flew as often as I could over the next few years, and eventually I set the women's altitude record.

Unfortunately, my father's finances took a turn for the worse after several years, and flying became a luxury he couldn't afford. I was devastated. Flying was my life — no; the best way to put it is that flying was all I had. It was the thing I looked forward to all day, that made me feel important and special.

There was more than that, though. I always felt there was something "up there" in the blue. When I was in the sky, I felt like an angel. I sometimes wondered what the Jewish heritage said about God, angels, and the next world. As the years went by, I felt an ever-strengthening desire to complete my truncated Jewish education. But where could I find the answer to my questions in Berkeley?

Eventually I worked out in my head that I had to make it back to New York, for two reasons: to rejoin the Jewish community, where I could learn more about Judaism, and to find someone who might sponsor my flights. Penny by penny I saved up, and as soon as I had the price of the ticket and a bit for food, I took off. As soon as I arrived in New York I managed to land a job as a social worker. Better yet, I met a Rebbetzin who also worked there part-time.

Rebbetzin Weinberg remembered my mother and grandmother from the Lower East Side, and she agreed to teach me some of the basics of Judaism, about God, and what the Torah says we ought to do, and about the next world. Eventually we got to talking about the unique role a Jewish woman plays in Jewish life. Those talks raised a lot of questions in my head.

I would have liked to spend more time with her, and ask some of my new questions, but everything changed after I answered an ad in the classified section of the New York Times. It asked for a female pilot.

A few days later a telegram arrived from a Mr. Busso, saying that he owned a chain of supermarkets called Path-Rite and was looking for some big publicity. He said he wanted to sponsor a flight across the Atlantic, and in order to really make the papers, he wanted a woman pilot for that flight, who would become the first woman to cross the Atlantic. Naturally, I jumped at his offer of an interview.

I still remember it. I came to see Mr. Busso in his posh office in Westchester. I walked into the office and saw a man sitting behind a huge oak desk. It must have been almost thirty feet from the door of the office just to reach that desk. After I walked in, he stood up and said, "Are you a pilot?"

I said, "Of course. I've been flying for some years now. I hold the women's altitude record."

For some reason he didn't seem too impressed. Instead, he brought me over to a coat rack in the front of the office, where a leather pilot's jacket hung. He took it off, handed it to me, and said, "Here. Try it on."

I usually didn't wear those things — I thought they were just for men. I usually liked to wear a sweatshirt and a skirt when I flew. But I tried on the jacket anyway. Oddly, Mr. Busso seemed more interested in how I looked in it than he was in my aviation skills. He had me turn around in the jacket as he rubbed his chin, then he pronounced. "It fits you well. You'll do. Would you like to go on that trip across the Atlantic?"

I couldn't believe my ears! I shrieked, "Yes!" but kept thinking the whole while, The jacket fits me, and that's why he selected me?

Before I could actually say anything he said, "I want you to sign a personal service contract with me. This flight will get great publicity for my stores, but I want you to agree to appear in public under my terms, and make personal appearances when I demand. I'm willing to compensate you nicely. Do we have a deal?"

I guess I should have been more careful before nodding my head, but I was so excited at being the first woman to cross the Atlantic that I wasn't thinking straight. He pulled a contract from the first drawer and said, "Good, just sign here, and we can begin tomorrow."

Without a moment's consideration I signed, and then Busso picked up the phone and made a few calls. After he hung up from the last one, he jotted down some information on a piece of paper and handed it to me. "Your first appointment," he said brusquely, "is at ten o'clock tomorrow morning in the theater district, 122 East Broadway, second floor, office 222, with Mrs. Smith. The next stop is the hair stylist. At one-thirty, you're to meet with the acting coach."

I didn't have time to think why I was told to have all these strange meetings. I had signed the contract; if this is what I had to do in order to fly again, I'd do it.

When I arrived at the address the next day, I was

surprised to read the sign on the office door: "Imagemak-ers." I wondered what that could be and just what I was supposed to do here? I walked in and said to the recep-tionist, "I have a ten o'clock appointment with Mrs. Smith."

She looked me up and down. "Your name?" she asked coldly.

"Emily Steinhart."

I guess the name didn't sound very important. "Are you sure you have an appointment with Mrs. Smith? Her services are in very high demand."

I thought, "Does she think I'm lying? I said, "Mr. Busso told me to come here at ten o'clock."

When she heard that name, suddenly her features changed. "Oh, Mr. Busso sent you. Please have a seat. Mrs. Smith is running a little bit behind schedule."

I took a seat and ruffled through a *Life* magazine. I had found an interesting article and barely noticed a man coming in a few minutes later. After speaking to the recep-tionist, he joined me in the waiting room.

He was short, with round glasses and a receding hair-line. He looked harmless enough, and I was burning up with curiosity. Maybe he could tell me what went on in this mysterious office. I asked him, by way of breaking the ice, "Are you ahead of me?"

He politely said, "No, I'm at ten-thirty."

"Can I ask you something?" I went on eagerly.

He smiled and said, "Certainly."

I asked him, "What is this place? I mean, I'm a pilot due to fly across the Atlantic and my sponsor told me to come here first."

He replied sympathetically, "Oh, no wonder you're confused. This place gives you a new name, and a new image for the public. Mrs. Smith is an expert at choosing the right name for you. Sometimes they also change your birthplace."

"Do you mean she's going to change my name?" I asked, astonished.

"Well, that depends on how your name sounds. What is it?"

"Emily Steinhart."

The man's mouth became a straight line, and he said thoughtfully, "Doesn't sound to me like such a bad name for a pilot. I guess it's all up to Mrs. Smith."

I asked him, "What do you do?"

"Right now I own a haberdashery store, but I'm planning on running for county judge in Jackson County, Missouri."

"Why do you want to change your name?"

He smiled again, and said, "I don't think Seymour McDibbs sounds very dashing."

"Even to be a county judge you have to change your name?"

"They say it's important if you plan on advancing in your field, especially in politics."

Just then the secretary announced, "Miss Steinhart? Mrs. Smith will see you now."

Thanking Mr. McDibbs, I walked into the inner office, where I found a hard-faced woman sitting motionless behind her desk with her elbows on it. In a business-like tone she told me to sit down. After a bit of small talk, she said, "Let me tell you why you're here. We specialize in remaking a person's image to appeal to the public. The first step is always the name. Now, what is yours, again?"

"Emily Steinhart."

Mrs. Smith giggled. "Oh, that just won't do! Let me get 'The Book.'"

I was about to ask her what "The Book" was, when I saw her get up from behind her desk and lug from the shelf a huge book, larger than any dictionary I've seen. She heaved it on to her desk and opened it; then I could tell it was a book full of nothing but names, categorized by field of endeavor.

"Now, we have to portray you with an image of someone young, daring, embarked on the ride of your life, and —"

At this point I couldn't help myself. "Excuse me, Ma'am, I'm not auditioning for Broadway. I'm just a pilot who wants to fly across the Atlantic."

Mrs. Smith looked at me and rolled her eyes. "I see you're new to this circuit. Anytime anyone gets his name in the papers, he usually comes to us or one of our competitors. It doesn't matter if it's politics, sports, aviation, or entertainment. We remake your past history and tell it to the press, and that makes your life so much more interesting."

I was stunned. "Do you mean people outside the entertainment industry also change their names?"

"Oh, the actors and singers are the only ones we let the public know about. It happens in just about every field.

Didn't you ever wonder why politicians and athletes, for example, never have weird or hard-to-pronounce names? How come no two public figures have the same name? In politics, you see, the name has to sound regal. I'm the one who suggested the name 'Woodrow Wilson.' It has a nice ring to it."

I was amazed. "That's not his real name?"

"Of course not. Did you think 'Barney Gruntwagen' could get elected? We also redid his birthplace, and even showed the press his 'hometown.' He really grew up in Hoboken, New Jersey.

"Now enough of this. I have a few suggestions for you, but first of all I've selected the name from 'The Book' that I think is best. It connotes a free, youthful spirit, and the fact that you're going on the ride of your life. I think 'Sally' is much more youthful than 'Emily,' don't you agree?"

More youthful? What? Was this woman out of her mind? I had trouble getting the next words out of my mouth. "Uh, Sally. Right. What's my last name?"

"Ride."

"Sally Ride?" I didn't like that. It sounded silly. "Um, couldn't you give me something closer to my real name?"

"You don't like 'Sally Ride'?" Mrs. Smith exhaled with a "humph." "Okay, I'll leave that one in 'The Book.' Maybe some other female aviator in the future will choose it."

Mrs. Smith wrote something down on her pad and continued, "I was certain that one was perfect for you, but I grant, you have to be comfortable with it too. Right, I'll send a memo across to our branches around the world that the name is still available. Now, what's your real name again?"

"Emily Steinhart," I said a little more forcefully.

"Well, if it has to be close to that... let me think." Suddenly Mrs. Smith got up and began to pace the room, every once in a while wiping her eyes behind her horn-rimmed glasses.

All of a sudden she stopped and pointed to the ceiling. "I've got it. Your last name will be Airport. Emily Airport!"

I giggled. Was this lady serious? "Um, doesn't that sound a bit like overdoing it?"

"Hmm... yes, perhaps you're right. What's your last name again?"

I blurted out, "Steinhart."

"That's it!"

"What's it?"

"Your heart is in the air. From now on your last name will be 'Airheart.' How's that?"

I said it a few times over to myself. I liked it. My heart was indeed in the air, and this name suited me.

"Emily Airheart," I said to Mrs. Smith.

"No, it won't do."

What? "I thought you said you liked it."

"No, Airheart is fine, but Emily is a name for an old lady. If you want, your new name can be close to your old name, but at the same time it must be unique."

Once again Mrs. Smith paced the room. I began to feel that she was the one who deserved to be on stage, more than the actors she picked names for. Abruptly she stopped and pointed again to the same spot on the ceiling. "I've got it!"

This time I was silent.

"You won't be Emily. Your name from now on is 'Emelia.'"

"Emelia?" I asked. "Is that a name?"

"It is and it isn't. Details aren't important, but it sounds like a European name I once heard, 'Emilio.' What matters is the sound: it evokes dashing, youth, and adventure-seeking. You may remember that some of the greatest early world explorers were Spanish and Italian. It's got the perfect ring."

I said "Emelia Airheart" to myself a few times. I liked the way it sounded. My thoughts were interrupted when I heard Mrs. Smith again. "Now, about your hometown. Where did you grow up?"

"What?" I asked in a daze. I was still settling into the fact that I'd have a new name.

"Where did you grow up?"

I answered mechanically, "The Lower East Side."

Mrs. Smith shook her head. "Good Lord, that won't do. We have to get you a more natural setting." This didn't make any sense at all: what was unnatural about the Lower East Side? But I never got the chance to ask the question; Mrs. Smith went on relentlessly, "You grew up in Kansas."

She ran behind her desk, opened an atlas, and started thumbing through it until, I guess, she came to a map of Kansas. As she studied the map she said, "I'm looking here for a town that..."

"I know, sounds right."

She pointed to small dot on the map. "Here — Lyndon! Perfect! Emelia Airheart, from Lyndon, Kansas. We'll tell the press about it, get you a new birth certificate and a photo of your hometown. If they want to interview your childhood friends, we'll supply some friends as well."

Mrs. Smith gave me some papers to sign. As I was signing, I heard her say under her breath, "Hmm... Lyndon. Might be a nice first name for someone who's in politics." She reached for "The Book" and wrote a line in it.

She took the papers back and handed me a carbon copy of each. I can tell you, I was glad to get out of there. I made it all the way to the street before I realized that I'd been in such a rush I had forgotten those papers Mrs. Smith gave me. I went back and said to the secretary, "I left some papers in the office."

Again in her cold voice, she answered, "I'm sorry, Mrs. Smith is consulting with a client right now. You'll have to wait until they're done."

"But I have to be at another appointment in ten minutes."

"Look, you forgot your papers, not me. Just sit and be patient."

I was very upset how she was treating me. I was going nowhere with her, so I thought a moment and said, "Mr. Busso gave me my next appointment, and if I show up late, I'll have to tell him it's because you made me wait."

That did it. The secretary turned pale, then quickly jumped up and knocked quietly on the office door. She opened it, and I saw Seymour McDibbs sitting where I'd sat, and once again Mrs. Smith was pacing the room. The secretary said softly, "Excuse me, Mrs. Smith, but...."

Mrs. Smith held up one finger, obviously a signal not to disturb her thoughts. She paced the room some more, then said, "Your new name must not only sound regal, it must also portray an image of impeccable honesty."

Once again she suddenly stopped moving and pointed to the ceiling. "I've got it! Your new name will be 'honest.' Harry Honest!"

Seymour said skeptically, "Harry Honest? That sounds like a con-man."

"Hmm... maybe you're right. What about Harry Truthful? No! Make that Harry True-Man... Harry Truman!"

Seymour smiled, and the secretary felt now she could interrupt. "That lady in here before —" she called to me, "what's your name?"

Instinctively I said, "Emily Steinhart."

"Miss Steinhart here forgot her papers."

Mrs. Smith simply pointed to her desk, where the papers sat. As the secretary went to get them, she called to me, "From now on, you're Emelia Airheart! Don't forget!"

I practically ran out of there, both to get away from this strange person and to make it to my next appointment on time. Fortunately, it was a professional hair stylist who was also located in the theater district. When I walked in, I noticed on the wall photos of many celebrities who must have been customers.

The secretary this time was a blond woman with long hair. She politely said, "May I help you?"

By now, I knew the magic words. "Mr. Busso sent me."

She smiled noncommittally. "Your name?"

"Emily Steinhart."

She looked at the appointment book. "Um, we just got a call that she canceled, and someone by the name of Emelia Airheart would be taking her place."

I thought, "She sure works quick!" But I just said, "Oh, that must be me. I'm Emelia Airheart."

The woman showed no sign of surprise; I figured she must be used to this sort of thing. "All right, please follow me."

I followed her into the salon, where she told me to sit down in a hairdresser's seat. I hadn't gone to beauty parlors much ever before. I usually brushed my hair and did the ponytail myself.

A hairstylist soon walked in, dressed in a pink vest. "My name is Mr. Zahn, and I understand Mr. Busso sent you."

I nodded.

"We're going to give you a new hairstyle for female pilots."

Before I could react, he cut off my long pony with one swipe of the scissors. Then he kept on cutting just about everywhere. I'd already figured I was supposed to have short hair, but this was ridiculous. I was about to object, but knew it wouldn't get me anywhere.

Finally he washed my hair over a sink and brushed it out. My hair looked like a mop: short, dry and wild. I looked like a grown-up tomboy. I didn't know if I should thank him or punch him in the stomach, but then I looked at my watch and saw I was due for my next appointment.

It was uptown, at the drama coach's apartment on the Upper West Side. I needed a taxi to make it on time, and they were nice enough to call one for me.

In the cab I had a second to reflect on what was happening. Busso was clearly out to make a complete new personality for me, one that he'd selected to fit with his scheme for his stores. I didn't know if I wanted to take part in this charade, but I knew I wanted to fly again, and I didn't see any alternative. Besides, I wasn't making money any other way, and the contract I signed did offer some lucrative terms. I swallowed hard, and when I looked up we were at the address.

By this time I had it down pat. I walked in and simply said to the person who answered the door, "Mr. Busso sent me. My name is Emelia Airheart." This time I got in right away.

The acting coach gave me lessons the rest of the afternoon, including how to walk like a man. I began to get the point: they were trying to give me a tomboy image — as if a woman couldn't possibly want to pilot a plane! I couldn't believe such stupidity. But I was stuck in this thing now, if only to make a living.

It was hard to get used to all the new things the coach was teaching me, but I did my best. We even started on how to hold a cigarette right, but when I told the man I'd never smoked in my life, he said that we'd better start that one tomorrow.

The next few days went by in a blur. I spent a lot of time with the acting coach, and when I wasn't doing that I was at other meetings. There was a costume designer for a new wardrobe, and a speaking trainer on how to make a speech in public and when to mention the PathRite Supermarket chain.

Several weeks later I made my first public appearance: a press conference, with two other pilots, about our upcoming flight. I was the center of attention. After all, the flight would make me the first woman to cross the Atlantic. I smiled as they had taught me, waved to the cameras, and made sure to mention PathRite stores when I was given a few minutes on the mike.

The big day finally arrived, and suddenly it turned out that I was only a back-up to the co-pilot. In all likelihood, I realized, I was to be nothing more than a passenger. Still, I was excited at being in the skies again.

Once the plane finally took off from Long Island, I felt that all the hassles I'd been through were worth it. I saw the ground fade away and then nothing but sky above. I felt free, broken loose from all bonds. There's a poem, written a little after my time, but all the pilots used to learn it by heart:

Oh, I have slipped the surly bonds of earth
And danced the sky on laughter-silvered wings...
It really was like that.

I leaned back into my seat, finally relaxed for the first time since Mr. Busso called. I wished the ride could go on for months. I felt so spiritual, so close to God.... Suddenly I sat bolt upright. I realized that with all my preparations for this adventure, I hadn't spoken even once to Rebbetzin Weinberg. Hopefully, once things settled down I'd meet with her again.

Almost thirty hours later the plane touched down in Burry Port, Wales. I couldn't believe the mob that was waiting for me. All my acting lessons came in handy as I waved and smiled just the right way. Later, when we went to London, another huge crowd greeted us. I felt a little sad for the co-pilots. They had done all the work and I was getting all the publicity.

We got back to New York by ocean liner. When I got back to my apartment I thought I would have a few days to recuperate. I was shocked when the very next day Mr. Busso called me and told me to be at the new store he was opening in New Rochelle. I told him I needed some time off, but he said I had to move quickly, as fame is not something that lasts too long. He told me to put on one of the flight costumes he'd had made for me. He was sending a beautician to my apartment to frizz up my hair and give me the impression of a tomboy once again.

The next few weeks were a whirlwind. If I wasn't attending a supermarket opening, I was giving an interview, shooting footage for newsreels, or giving speeches — always mentioning PathRite stores. Eventually I realized that I couldn't take much more of the madness. I called Busso, thinking I'd just tell him straight out that I had to have a few days off. Surprisingly, his secretary told me he was away in Sicily on business, and I should speak to his assistant, Mr. Pellegrino. When I told him how tired I was, Mr. Pellegrino was far more sympathetic than Busso would have been, and let me take a few days off.

Finally, some rest! After some serious sleep, I thought about Rebbetzin Weinberg. Since I'd started all this business I hadn't had a chance to speak with her, so I gave her a call. She'd heard about some new female pilot, but had no idea it was me. Right away she invited me to her home in the Lower East Side for that Shabbos. Suddenly I was happy that I could get out of those leather pilot jackets and dungarees I always had to wear. I could dress the way I wanted to, like a woman. I just wanted to be myself.

I got a shock when I walked into the Weinberg's apartment. There seemed to be kids all over the place! It was pretty small, and certainly crowded, but every corner radiated warmth. I saw how the Rebbetzin stayed calm in the middle of the raging Battle of the Kids, and I, the fearless pilot, envied her nerves. I only had to deal with airplanes; she dealt with real people.

She spent a lot of time with me that Shabbos, and told me all about my grandmother and mother. I told her about all the stuff they made me go through, and how I was now officially "Emelia Airheart."

She said, "Never mind that, what's your real name?"

I said, "Emily Steinhart."

She smiled. "Not that name. Your Hebrew name."

"Esther Beileh."

"From now on, at least in this house, that's what I'll call you."

I felt sad when Rabbi Weinberg made *havdalah*. It meant back to the cigarettes, flight jacket, and trying to be a pretend man. I reminded myself that this was my only way to be where I loved to be, in the air. It still rankled: this wasn't *me*. I rationalized it all by telling myself I was just playing a role, and that I knew who I really was. If

Busso wanted me to play-act, and was going to pay me for it, I could put up with it, I thought. Deep inside, though, I felt like a freak. And in just a few days, the public appearances were grating at my nerves so much that I began to feel like a circus performer.

Thankfully, Busso noticed the crowds thinning, a sure sign that interest in me was waning, so he decided I needed another flight (which he referred to as a "stunt"). He decided I would duplicate Lindbergh's flight, or close to it, so becoming the first woman to cross the Atlantic solo. When I said I didn't think I could do a thirty-hour flight alone, Mr. Pellegrino told me that Lindbergh had flown from New York to Paris, and I would only have to go from Newfoundland to Ireland by the shortest possible route. So, a few months later, in celebration of Lindbergh's feat, I took off from Harbour Grace, Newfoundland amongst cheering crowds.

Once again, the minute I was airborne I had a feeling of euphoria. To add to it, finally I was alone and nobody could bother me! I thought how the press was going to make me into a heroine once again. Then I thought about Rebbetzin Weinberg. What was I doing that was really so heroic? Well, I was crossing the Atlantic in an airplane, just to be the first woman to do it. Okay, that was something heroic, but my trip would be over in thirty hours. My heroics would end when I touched down in Northern Ireland. In contrast, Rebbetzin Weinberg was on the job twenty-four hours a day, seven days a week. To add to that, she wasn't getting any publicity and she wasn't making any money at her job. It certainly cost her plenty! She was the one building the Jewish nation; I was just flying a silly airplane over a body of water.

I began to wonder how much longer I wanted to do this. I was realizing, slowly, that there are other kinds of adventures, ones that don't involve popping flash bulbs and toasts in champagne. Did I really want to fly my whole life? But when would it end? Would Busso ever leave me in peace? If he didn't, I could never discover the adventure of launching a family. How much longer would I have to wear this flight jacket? Suddenly it seemed so ridiculous. Why did I have to wear men's clothing? I wasn't a man. If Busso dressed up like a woman he'd be a laughingstock. So why did I have to do opposite?

These thoughts kept swirling through my head all the time I was in the sky. When I landed in Northern Ireland I felt depressed — it was back to playing heroine again. I was used to the cheering crowds by now and I knew what to say to the reporters while maintaining my fake smile, coupled with some signs of fatigue from my grueling flight. Ho hum.

Once I got back to New York, it was the supermarket-and-speaking tour once again. Busso had me working non-stop: he always had some new campaign or idea to follow up on, just to make him some more money. The only time it ever let up was when his assistant, Pellegrino, took over. He at least was halfway a human being.

A few months later Busso was gone for what seemed like a long time. When I asked Mr. Pellegrino what had happened and where Mr. Busso was, he said someone had shot at him while he was eating in a restaurant, and he was now recovering in the hospital. "It must have been one of his former employees," I thought bitterly. At the time I didn't understand what this said about Busso's "business" dealings.

Since I had some time off, I started learning all I could with the Weinbergs. The Rebbetzin introduced me to some other members of her shul. Eventually I even moved to the Lower East Side, to be closer to the Jewish community. Very few people recognized me as I walked the streets there, since I made sure to wear long sleeves and a long dress. I finally felt that I was the way I was supposed to be — I could be a woman.

Unfortunately, Busso soon returned, and with him the grind. Appearances, speeches, store openings, interviews, and whenever the public began to get bored with me, another heroic flight to recapture their imagination. My only escape from the madness was when I could spend Shabbos with the Weinbergs. As provisions for one of my flights — the first non-stop from Newark to Mexico City — she even gave me some gefilte fish to take with me.

After that flight I decided that I had had enough of this schizophrenic existence. Here I was, wearing long sleeves and dresses on my time off, and the next day wearing a flight jacket and pretending to smoke. (I never did manage to inhale the horrible stuff.) I didn't want to be Emelia Airheart anymore. I just wanted to be plain old Emily Steinhart again. If it meant not flying any more, well, I was about ready to go on to a better kind of adventure.

I mustered up my strength and told Busso I needed a break from flying. Surprisingly, he said I could take a two-week vacation, but when I told him I wanted to take off six months to a year, he flew into a rage. He needed my help, it seems, to promote some new stores he'd opened in Queens. He had a considerable amount invested, and couldn't risk losing me that long just "for my sentimentalities," as he put it. He told me there would be serious financial repercussions if I quit on him now.

I had no choice but to go back on the circuit. I later set another record, flying from Hawaii to LA non-stop. But the next week I felt very fatigued, and I knew it wasn't just from the flight. I actually had trouble getting out of bed in the morning — because I dreaded putting on that flight jacket, and the smell of cigarette smoke nauseated me. I started to appear in public unkempt, arriving late, even missing meetings with reporters. I began to talk softly, and looked at the ground as I walked. When I came home, I sometimes burst into tears for no apparent reason.

It came to a head in December, when I was scheduled to appear at the Grand Opening of Busso's new store in Fresh Meadows. I was supposed to be there at ten, but that morning I just couldn't get out of bed. For the last few days my limbs had felt heavy, and that morning it was as if I was carrying twenty-five pounds on my shoulders.

When I overslept the Fresh Meadows opening, Busso came to my apartment in the Lower East Side. "Do you realize," he screamed, "the damage you've caused me? You made a fool out of me. I promised the public a glimpse at famous aviator Emelia Airheart, and you don't show up? Try this one more time and you'll be back as a social worker. I can find plenty of girls that fit that flight jacket."

I surprised myself when I said, "Go ahead."

That caught him. He knew it wasn't going to be easy to build a new star. Suddenly his features hardened, and he seemed dark and cold. "Don't try anything," he said. "Anyone who double-crosses me sincerely regrets it. Perhaps you think that when my last star died, it was an accident?"

I was shocked. He had used Olympic skater Debbie Hannel for years before me, and one day she was found dead in her apartment. The police had called it accidental death.

"She also wanted to take some time off," snarled Busso. "Don't make the same mistake. I expect you to give an extra long appearance in Fresh Meadows tomorrow. I hope you won't disappoint me."

He saw the look of terror on my face and said, "Just do as I say, and everything will be fine. I hope this Rabbi's wife you've been hanging around with lately isn't putting strange ideas in your head. I wouldn't want anything to happen to her either."

I tried to appear calm, and forced a smile — that was something I'd gotten good at. But I knew I had to do something, and fast. Busso seemed to read my mind, though. As he walked out the door he said, "And don't try to run away. Wherever you go, I'll find you. People who double-cross me don't live too long." He walked out and slammed the door.

I was terrified. What had I gotten myself into? I should have realized a long time ago that Busso was involved with the mob. Now I could only admit to myself that there was no way out. None, at least, unless I could come up with a plan good enough to fool him.

A few days later I put on my cleanest flight jacket and strode confidently into Busso's office. I told him I'd like to try the ultimate "stunt": I would be the first woman to fly solo around the world. He liked the idea — I guess he knew it would be great publicity for his stores. When I told him I needed a new custom-built plane to make such a long flight, at first he was about to yell at me again, but quickly I told him that I'd already put down a deposit on a new Boeing Condor. I wanted to pay for this plane and have it as my own. That calmed him down.

Busso immediately got his team together to plan the campaign. I'd require refueling stops along the way, caches of provisions, local contact people, and lots more. In the meantime I put in all the personal appearances he scheduled and did everything else he asked of me. Secretly, I also met with the Rebbetzin. She helped me with all the details of my plan.

I was sick of the marching bands and streamers, but when I flew off in early May from Miami to Natal, Brazil, I had once again to put on the fake smile for the cameras.

The course they had given me lay close to the equator, which meant I could stay over land as much as possible. It almost went wrong, though, because on that first leg, from Miami to Brazil, I started thinking of carrying out my plan prematurely. But I knew that if I didn't do it properly it might fail, so I continued on my trip. From Natal I crossed the ocean in about 13 hours, and landed in St. Louis, Senegal. On the next leg I briefly flew over the mouth of the Red Sea, and how I longed then to stop in on Israel!

But I knew the time wasn't right yet.

I really enjoyed the solitude of being up in the sky, although since I had never made anything nearly as long as this trip before, at times I was bored and cramped. I was glad I had bought the new Condor: it was large enough that I could stand up and shuffle around a bit in the cabin, with one finger on the wheel, at times when the rudder didn't demand my full attention. By the end of June I had made it to Darwin Lae, New Guinea. From there, my next stop for refueling was at Howland Island in the Pacific, then I would fly on to Hawaii. From there I would take the last leg to complete my trip and touch down, fittingly, where I saw my first airplane: Oakland, California.

I had known all along that the longest leg of my trip over water would be the stretch from New Guinea to Howland Islands. Here it was, coming up. Now was the right time to execute my escape plan.

Once I was over the ocean, I sent a radio signal that I was low on fuel. After that I made no more radio contact. They thought, naturally, that I was in trouble. I ignored all their attempts to contact me. After a few days they sent out a search party, and eventually, to my embarrassment, the Seventh Fleet came to search for me or the remains of my plane. What they couldn't have guessed is that I had turned the plane around in a wide sweep and landed again in a remote corner of New Guinea.

It's amazing how much you can accomplish by showing a wad of dollars, especially if you're showing it to poor natives. I offered them what must have been six months' salary in return for their help.

The first thing I asked for was a refueling. I had landed at a dirt airstrip surrounded by jungle, but they did have gasoline (in return for dollars). They hid me and the plane in the hut they called a hangar, while some others quickly painted my airplane over. I was surprised how fast they worked. Soon I was ready for the next stage of my plan. I gave each native a final bribe, making them promise never to reveal they had seen me — but it was unlikely anyone would look for me back in New Guinea. They all thought I was lost in the ocean.

You know, I never thought it would be a problem when they found no trace of me or my plane. After all, the Pacific is a very large place. I had no idea what a hullabaloo they would make about it.

I simply followed the same route I had taken coming. The money I had saved over the years came in handy: I could buy assistance from anyone. Outside of the remote New Guinea jungle it wasn't safe to tell the truth and offer a bribe; the lure of newspaper fame would have been overpowering. But I had this part of the plan worked out perfectly. In most cases it wasn't even necessary to tell any outright lies. The repainted plane was unrecognizable, and I knew how to act like a man. My short hair and aviator's clothing completed the deception. Most people don't look beyond the surface, you know, or look behind a plain story. I simply told the airfield people I had come in on a short flight from a neighboring city to pick up some cargo. If anyone wondered why I was taking off without loading anything on the plane, I simply told them there was a mix-up. The goods had been shipped to the wrong port —

which naturally was my next refueling stop. I followed the route until, *baruch Hashem*, I landed the plane at the airfield in Lod, what is now called Ben Gurion Airport.

I stored my plane in one of the hangars in Lod, and right away became Emily Steinhart again. Soon I met with the people that Rebbetzin Weinberg had suggested. I was glad to walk the streets and not have people look at me! I could *daven* at the Western Wall any time I wanted to, and didn't have Busso or his gang of hoodlums to worry about — only the Arab toughs, and let me tell you, they were nothing compared to Busso. At last I read in the newspapers that everyone had given up hope of finding me, concluding I had crashed in the Pacific. I wasn't about to explain to anyone why they never found any trace of my plane.

I decided after only a short while that I never wanted to leave this holy Land. I've been here since 1937, and thank God married a wonderful husband and was able to raise my children in peace.

Katz and Hecker looked at each other. What a story! Katz spoke first: "What happened with your airplane?"

"Oh, yes. Between buying the plane, and paying for aid and fuel all the way back, after a few years I was short on cash, so I had to sell the plane. I guess I should have had it repainted again first. The reason the paint is wearing off is that it's the rush job I had done in New Guinea, where I'm sure they didn't have the high-quality paints you could get in America."

Mrs. Kroningsburg took on a serious look. "You both need to know, I believe Busso is still involved with the mob and as ruthless as ever, although I hear he's no longer in supermarkets. That is why I asked for your complete cooperation. And that's why you cannot breathe a word of this to anyone."

Katz sat there in shock. He didn't know what to say, so he just nodded.

Without saying a word, Esther Beileh got up from her seat, removed the reel of tape from the recorder, and went to the desk in the corner of the room. She took a fading manila envelope off her desk, came back to the couch, and spilled the contents on the coffee table. She explained what each document was: her birth certificate, the name-change documents Mrs. Smith had given her, her receipt for the Boeing Condor, and various other documents proving that her story was authentic.

"The procedure will be as follows," she announced. "After my demise, you will receive this tape and all these documents. I will instruct that they be delivered to you in Be'er Sheva. You will be free to examine them, and if they meet your approval you will sign this document acknowledging receipt."

Katz and Hecker got up to leave, but before they could take a step, Esther Beileh said, "Remember, not a word to anyone."

Hecker said, "Don't worry."

Katz took a step to the door, when Esther Beileh said, "Mr. Katz, I have one small favor to ask of you."

"Sure, what is it?"

"I'd like to see my plane one more time."

Katz smiled, and said, "It's in the service hangar just now — this all got started when we tried to peel the paint off of it. I'll keep it under wraps, but you can come to see it any time you'd like."

Esther Beileh escorted the two to the door. She seemed relieved to have gotten the story out, but at the same time, Hecker could tell in her eyes that she seemed sad. Her expression turned from her usual bright smile to withdrawn. She murmured "I'll be in touch," but so softly that Katz and Hecker could barely hear her. Afterwards she rubbed her eyes, and as the door was closing Katz noticed her taking a tissue to her eyes.

The next Chol HaMoed Sukkos, Esther Beileh and her whole family came to Be'er Sheva. Katz wanted to give Esther Beileh an exclusive tour of the Condor, even to let her sit in the pilot's seat one more time. She declined, and simply said she wanted to see it as a normal tourist. She was with her whole family of children and grandchildren, she told him, and didn't want to draw extra attention.

Since it was Chol HaMoed and Esther Beileh wanted only to be part of a tour, Katz had no choice but to display (possibly for the last time in her lifetime) the old Condor. It would just be part of the tour.

Katz spotted Esther as she casually approached the weather-beaten airplane with the paint half peeled off. He studied her features from a distance. The eyes opened in awe, but then they quickly turned cold and dark. It was as if Esther wanted to forget her past the very moment it was here in front of her.

Hecker once again gave his speech to the crowd: "This Boeing Condor 14C is badly in need of refurbishing, as you can see. It's one of the few still in existence today. Famed female aviator Emelia Airheart flew this same model of plane on her last fatal flight, an attempt to be the first woman to circle the globe solo. She probably ran out of fuel and crashed into the Pacific. No trace of her wreckage was ever found." Katz was standing off to the side, and couldn't help notice Esther Beileh sneak a smile with her husband.

Following Sukkos the Condor was put back into storage. As Katz put a sheet over it and locked the hangar, he wondered when he could pull this Condor out once again and show it in all its glory.

He went about his business of running the museum. He felt gruesome waiting for somebody to die before his treasure could be unveiled, but what choice did he have? He called the Kroningsburgs before Pesach and asked if Esther wanted to see her plane again, or perhaps make a trip just with her husband so she could sit at the controls one more time. She politely declined. Six months turned into a year, and Katz called before every Sukkos and Pesach. He realized that his true intent was to make sure Esther Beileh Kroningsburg hadn't passed away without him knowing about it.

It was eight years now. Esther celebrated her sixty-fifth birthday in 1970. By now Katz was calling only once a year, sometimes simply hanging up when he heard her voice answering, demonstrating that she wasn't yet dead.

After Katz acquired an exemplar of the airplane Israel used to bomb the Iraqi nuclear reactor in 1981, he called Esther and invited her to see it. She declined.

By 1991 he was no longer able to call and hang up when he heard her voice — he was afraid of the new caller ID. That year Azriel Hecker accepted a job at Wayne State University in Indiana and moved to *chutz la'aretz*. They'd never spoken much about the secret that only they knew.

In 1993 Katz received a shocking phone call. Hecker had suddenly passed away from a heart attack, at the age of 58. After the *levayah* in Be'er Sheva, a foreboding sense of loneliness enveloped Katz. He was now the only one alive who knew the secret. Frantically he pulled out the papers and checked the wording. He had to find a way to pass the secret on to someone else. Then, reading over the fine print, he froze in horror. Here was something he hadn't taken seriously when he signed in 1962, but the words were very clear. If he and Hecker should both pass away before Esther Beileh, the plane was to be destroyed. And there was nothing he could do to stop it from happening.

In his wildest dreams Katz hadn't thought that the plane would still be sitting in its hangar, covered with the same sheet, hidden from the outside world, after the turn of the century. Yet it was the year 2001 now. "She must be, what, 96 by now," he thought bemusedly. "I guess it pays to stay in shape."

Finally, in June 2003 Katz got the call he was no longer even waiting for. Esther Beileh Kroningsburg had just passed away in Sha'arei Tzedek hospital, at the age of 98. He dropped everything and sped to Bayit VaGan for the *levayah*.

He came back to the museum that same day, tired from all the driving. It was beyond belief: forty-one years had passed since that strange day. He was twenty pounds heavier than he'd been then, and had lost all his hair. But he would have aviation's biggest secret unveiled, at last.

A week later his phone rang, and someone called Yoni Kroningsburg was on the line. What...? Oh, Esther Beileh's son! "Of course, the family just got up from *shiv'ah*," he thought. Yoni explained that he was coming to Be'er Sheva tomorrow in order to deliver a package.

"Tomorrow...." was Katz's only coherent thought.

Katz was literally sitting on his hands, looking at the clock every few minutes, waiting for Yoni's arrival. He had waited forty-one years for this day, yet he felt as anxious as he had on the day of his wedding.

At exactly eleven-thirty in the morning there was a knock on the door. Katz buzzed it open, and in walked a man wearing a black hat and black suit, carrying an envelope. His hair was a bit long and untidy, and to Katz he looked tired. Well — not surprising.

"*Shalom aleichem*," the man said. "My name is Yoni Kroningsburg. I'm Esther Beileh's son. I was instructed to bring you this package," and he dropped it on Katz's desk.

Even though forty-one years had elapsed, Katz recognized the envelope. Surprisingly, it looked to be in almost the same condition he remembered it when it was sealed all those years ago. He ripped it open the way a child unwraps a candy bar, and dumped the contents on his desk. It all seemed to be in order. There were the photos, the birth certificate, and most importantly, the reel of tape. "I'll have to transfer this to cassette," he thought. "Wow, better get an expert, the tape must be brittle after so many years." He asked Yoni to wait a few moments while he examined each item. After a few moments he looked up and smiled. It was all there.

A more serious look crossed Katz's face as he said, "Sorry to hear about your mom. She was a more special woman than you knew, and accomplished some great things."

Yoni didn't respond to this, only said in a monotone voice, "Are the contents correct?"

"Yes, it's all here," Katz said as he leaned back in his chair.

"You have to sign here acknowledging receipt, and then we will have fulfilled our part of the agreement."

Katz quickly grabbed the gold pen from his penholder and signed his name, and with a broad grin gave Yoni the paper. Yoni folded it and put it into his jacket pocket.

Katz expected Yoni to turn for the door. Instead he did the opposite. He put his knuckles on the desk top and leaned over it, looking Katz in the eye. "Now that the paper's been signed, I want to tell you something. I know all about my mother's career as an aviator in the 1930s."

Katz squinted, and his mouth became a circle. "You

know?" he faltered.

"A few days before my mother passed away, she called me into her hospital room. Although she was in her late nineties, she was coherent until her last day. She told me all about her life as Emelia Airheart, and how she made this agreement with you forty-one years ago."

Katz sat there listening with an unmoving face. He was in shock. Yoni looked down at Katz and said softly, "My mother had a final wish before she left this world."

Katz was curious. "What is it?"

Yoni said, quietly but forcefully, "She asked me to come here and request in her name that you not tell anyone about her life as Emelia Airheart."

Katz felt as if he'd been run over by a Concorde. Did he hear that correctly? Finally he managed to blurt out, "What? I've waited forty-one years to tell the world!"

Yoni said, "I realize that. But Mama told me on her deathbed that she was ashamed of wearing those pants and flight jacket, and asks you as her dying wish not to reveal to anyone what you know."

Katz sat there in shock. He had kept his part of the agreement, and now this bombshell. He tried to hide the anger in his voice, without much success. "I'm sorry, I have a written contract that clearly states—"

Yoni lifted a hand. "I know I have no legal backing for what I'm asking. Mama knew that too. You're entirely within your rights. If you choose to publicize what you know, I will have no hard feelings towards you. But — it was my mother's dying wish that she remain unrevealed. Mr. Katz, she was abused during her life. Please, I ask you, respect her wishes and don't abuse her now that she's gone."

"But I have that airplane...."

"You still have the airplane, Mr. Katz. I'm not asking to take that away from you. Paint it over, please, and let no one else know what it really was. I'm only repeating my mother's dying wish. Please, try to listen."

Katz sat back in his chair. This was too much. Forty-one years, and now this? He got up and looked out the window of his office. In the distance he could see the Condor's hangar.

Finally, he said, "I don't understand. Your mother left a life of fame and success to come to Israel, in 1937, to lead a religious life. Revealing what I know would only perpetuate her memory. Look what she had, look what she gave up! I'm not religious, you know, but isn't that something really special? They call it... what's the name... a *kiddush haShem!*"

Yoni took a step away from the desk. "Even if I agreed with you, which incidentally I do, it makes no difference. This was my mother's dying wish, and I'm here to try my best to carry it out. I can only appeal to your Jewish heart. Let Emelia Airheart's legend live on, and let my mother rest in peace."

Katz was at a loss for words. All he could make out was, "I'll think about it, and let you know my decision."

"You don't have to let us know. Should you publicize the story, we'll know about it right away: I'm sure the press will hound us in a way that mother never knew. I just hope you can see things my way." Silently Yoni stood up and walked out of the office.

Katz sat down again at his desk for a few moments. He couldn't move a muscle. Finally, he found his hands and turned on the computer by his desk. He went to his address book and looked under "P." Two numbers sat there, one on top of the other. The first one, under "Painter," was Yair Posner, who usually refurbished and repainted his older planes. Just below it, under "Post," was his friend Yaakov Black, a reporter from the Jerusalem Post who occasionally did stories about the Museum's newest attraction.

Katz sat looking at both numbers. He felt his hands shaking. He looked up and down. Which one should he call? One number would bring a worldwide attraction, possibly fame and wealth for his museum. The other would respect a woman's dying wish.

He looked at both for what seemed to be an eternity. His heart was racing and his teeth chattering. Finally he couldn't take it any longer. He picked up the phone and called one of the numbers.

Shmuel Katz liked Chol HaMoed Sukkos. It was good for business. It seemed that the only time most people wanted to see his Air Force aviation museum was during Chol HaMoed Pesach and Sukkos. He always hired extra guides during those two weeks. Although he now walked with a cane, nonetheless he mixed with the crowd, and listened as the guide pointed to the Boeing Condor.

"This plane recently received a fresh coat of paint and has been refurbished. It is a Boeing Condor 14C, one of the few remaining in the world today. It was this same model of plane that the legendary American aviator Emelia Airheart flew when she disappeared in 1937 in her attempt to become the first woman to fly around the world solo. Most experts believe she simply ran out of fuel and crashed in the Pacific. No trace of her plane has ever been found."

Coming Attractions

When Chaim heard the doorbell, he reluctantly hit the Off button on the remote control. He managed to untwist his unwilling body, and succeeded in getting up from his recliner to answer the door. He looked at his watch and thought, "Exactly nine-thirty. He's as punctual as ever."

Chaim walked to the entranceway, opened the door, and saw the smiling face of Rabbi Goodman. The graying beard suddenly stood out in Chaim's gaze; his teacher seemed to have aged between visits. Chaim now noticed that he was standing awkwardly, as if the weight of his attaché case was tugging on his right arm.

"Come in, Rabbi. Can I take your coat?"

Rabbi Goodman walked in and took off his coat and handed it to Chaim. After Chaim hung it up, Rabbi Goodman said a polite, "Thank you." Automatically he followed Chaim back into the living room. Chaim motioned him to have a seat, and Rabbi Goodman gently sat down on the couch. After a moment, he sat up rigidly and put the attaché case on his lap. Chaim took his regular Lazy Boy recliner, swiveling it to face his guest.

Rabbi Goodman, with the same genuine smile on his face, said, "How's your wife?"

Chaim said, "Baruch Hashem, Miriam's fine."

"How old are your children now?"

"Tehillah is almost eight, and Suri is four and a half. Can I get you something hot to drink?"

"No thank you, I've got to make a lot of calls tonight,

so I'll get right to the point. Baruch Hashem, the yeshivah has taken in over seventy-five new students this year, and we're overcrowded and understaffed. In some cases we've been forced to put over forty boys in a class. It's gotten so crowded that we've had to buy several temporary classrooms. In addition, new government regulations have obliged us to install a sprinkler system; fine and good, but it cost us over ten thousand dollars. I didn't anticipate all these added expenses when I made the budget for this year, but what could I do? Turn away someone who wants to learn by us?"

Rabbi Goodman leaned forward, and said in a soft voice, "I don't say this to everyone, but we're two months behind with our payroll."

His features became serious as his eyes began to sparkle with determination. "Do you think you could do a little better than last year?"

Chaim didn't blink. After another concerted effort he successfully pulled himself out of the recliner and walked off. While he was gone, Rabbi Goodman stared blankly at the TV in the center of the room.

Chaim soon returned and handed the rabbi a check. Rabbi Goodman stood up, and against his usual custom he opened it and took a peek. His eyes grew wide and he smiled widely. "Thank you, Chaim. Let me write you a receipt."

He sat down quickly, put the attaché case back on his lap, opened it and took out the receipt book. He seemed accustomed to using the top of his attaché case as his "desk." After he wrote the receipt he stood up and handed it to Chaim.

Chaim took a step towards the front door, hoping that The Topic wouldn't come up this time. He was mistaken.

Rabbi Goodman gave a quick gaze at the TV and said simply, "You really should get rid of it."

Chaim faked innocence. "What?"

"That thing that plays the videos."

Chaim smiled, and said with pride, "Actually, we switched to DVD a few years ago. It's a much better system. You don't have to wait to fast forward, you can pick the scene you like and go to it right away, and you also get outtakes and...."

Rabbi Goodman quickly lifted his hand. "I don't care what you call it. You use it to watch Hollywood movies, right?"

Chaim reluctantly responded, "Only kosher ones."

Rabbi Goodman quickly countered, "You mean ones that aren't so *treifeh*. There's no such thing as kosher ones."

Chaim appeared flustered briefly, and said with a bit of whining in his voice, "Look, Rebbe, I'll be honest with you. The *heimische* bus leaves at seven-thirty in the morning; even then, without traffic I can just make it to the office before nine. Some nights, it's not so unusual for me to get home past ten o'clock, and I haven't eaten dinner yet. After a day like that, my only escape is to sit down here in front of the TV— I mean DVD — and watch something. It takes my mind off the daily grind."

Rabbi Goodman cringed. "TV? Is that thing also a television set, besides a video player?"

After a few moments of silence, Chaim said, "Well, I use it to watch a cable channel for TV classics. It only shows programs from the fifties and sixties." Suddenly Chaim's features lit up. "Wait a second. You had a TV in your house when you were growing up. I'm watching the same things you watched, and you turned out okay, so it can't be all bad."

Rabbi Goodman looked at the floor for a moment and then said, "It's true we owned a TV when I grew up in Baltimore, but back then we didn't realize the danger yet. We thought of it simply as a radio with a picture tube. We didn't realize the addiction, and the way the programs linger in your head. With radio we had to use our imagination, so a lot of the impact came from within. With television it's the opposite. The images are sent to you full and complete, and you have no say over what gets in to your head. That's why I encourage the parents of the children in my school to get rid of their TVs."

Chaim looked puzzled. "Why?"

Rabbi Goodman said, "Do you know what it's like to teach *mishnayos* to a boy after he's been watching a giant purple dinosaur sing and dance on TV? To him the Mishnah is dull black and white. The Mishnah doesn't sing and doesn't dance. But the Mishnah is *emess,* and the dinosaur is *sheker.* It's an overweight *goy* in a dinosaur costume. Only once the faked-up image gets in his head, it's hard to compete with."

"Well, for kids. The DVD doesn't affect me."

Rabbi Goodman just gave a slight smile. "That's just the danger: it does. TV and video have the same impact on an adult mind, only it's subtler." Chaim stirred restlessly, and Rabbi Goodman raised his hand. "Let me ask you something. Let's say you learn a number of *mishnayos* when you get home from work. Then you put the kids to bed, and when you come back from Maariv you put on your TV, I mean DVD, and relax by watching a hopefully *pritzus*-free 1950s movie. The next day at Shacharis and on the bus, what do you think about? The movie or the *mishnayos?* You know which. The movie fed living images into your head, and there's nothing you can do to get rid of them."

Chaim was silent. He knew the Rabbi was right, at least about this point. Last night he'd picked up a classic DVD from Blockbuster, and stayed up so late that in the morning he missed the *heimische* bus again. He was forced to drive his car into the city. All the while he was driving he ran over scenes from the movie in his head, wondering "what would have happened if he'd said this, or done that." He ran through every event in the movie this way, looking for flaws in the plot, and asking — well, *kushyos.* Chaim realized that he'd been treating the movie as if its script were a page of Gemara. He suddenly felt queasy. What was happening to him?

But in a moment he got a grip on himself. He spoke up and said, "Look, I don't have time nowadays to learn the way I did in yeshivah. When I was younger...."

Those words suddenly rang in the Rabbi's ears as if he were standing next to a clanging Liberty Bell. "When I was younger...." His mind began to show its own video flashback. In an instant a fog enveloped Chaim. No longer did

Rabbi Goodman see the heavyset father of two standing before him. In his place stood a slightly overweight yeshivah-*bachur.* He remembered that conversation word for word.

"You must go to Eretz Yisrael," he was telling young Chaim. "There are far less distractions." Then the scene switched to the lunchroom, with Rabbi Goodman standing off at a distance while Chaim astounded everyone at his table with his fluency in TV trivia. Years later he could still remember lines from movies. Rabbi Goodman overheard Chaim fighting it out over a scene in *Superman II,* until the other *bachur* finally admitted that Chaim's version was correct.

The *bachur* said, "Wait a second. I saw that movie a few weeks ago on TV when I was home in LA for the break. When did you see it? Did you rent the video?"

Chaim shook his head. "Actually, I saw that one only once, when it came out."

The *bachur* looked at Chaim, amazed. He counted on his fingers and said, "That was twelve years ago!"

That was when Rabbi Goodman realized that Chaim had a gift. It was a difficult one to apply, though. Put simply, Chaim remembered pictures much better than he did words. Unfortunately, the Vilna Shas didn't have many pictures.

Rabbi Goodman had already, back then, noticed something else. Chaim loved neon. When they went on a bus together from Lakewood to the Port Authority terminal, the two "spoke in learning" most of the way. But often a neon sign would distract Chaim, so much so that he would stop dead in the middle of learning to stare at it briefly. By the time the bus reached New York City, Chaim was taking more and more peeks out the window. Anything bright and flashy attracted his young mind. "This young mind is brilliant, but so delicate and easily distracted," Rabbi Goodman thought. And as he well knew, there is nothing as bright and flashy as television.

He often mentioned to Chaim why we say twice a day in Shma that we should not go after our heart and our eyes. We mustn't be impressed by surface things; we have to delve deeper to find the *emess*, as we do in a page of Gemara, not in a TV show.

The fog of the past cleared from Rabbi Goldman's eyes, and once again the 250-pound, forty-two-year-old Chaim stood in front of him. For a moment, the Rabbi saw a failure, all his hard work in vain. Yes, Chaim supported his yeshivah, had a good job, a nice family, and lived in Monsey. But the sight of that TV made Rabbi Goodman feel sick. He knew Chaim didn't stand a chance with it in the house.

Rabbi Goodman's eyes focused, and he once again gave Chaim his full attention.

"...I used to sit in the Beis Midrash for two whole *sedarim*, but I don't have the time or the patience for that any more. The trip to Manhattan is grueling enough. I need to relax at night, not hunch over a Gemara."

Rabbi Goodman paused and looked at Chaim again. "It's never too late for him," he thought as he managed to say, "I have only one simple suggestion. Take along a tape of *daf yomi, parashah*, or whatever. Listen to it on the bus or in the car before you get to the office. Try to make a picture out of the *daf,* and keep that image in your mind. I have a *talmid* who does that, and is able to recall one thing on each *daf.* For example, on *daf beis* of Masechta Sukkah, which talks about a sukkah over forty *amos* high, he pictures a giant sukkah with first base in it. Try to picture a few of the words you hear, and dwell on that in your spare moments, not the movie you saw last night. Images stay in your mind forever, and you can't get rid of them. At least try to make them positive images."

Chaim looked at his watch abruptly and said, "Don't you have other calls to make tonight?"

Rabbi Goodman nodded yes and said sadly, "I really should be going."

After they walked together out of the den and to the entranceway, Chaim took the Rabbi's coat out of the closet and handed it to him. He walked him out the door, waved good-bye, and watched him get in his car and drive away. He couldn't help the fleeting thought, "Phew, I'm sure glad he's gone." Walking now with a lively step, Chaim went right back into the den, collapsed onto the recliner and hit the On button on the remote control. He surfed through the channels, and stopped when he found a rerun of "Star Trek: The Next Generation." Midway through the show, Chaim thought he heard something, but didn't look up. Only during the next commercial he noticed Miriam sitting on the couch with some packages from Macy's.

"Wanna see what I bought?" she asked.

Chaim feigned interest. "Uh, okay."

She showed him her shoes and new bracelet, but by the

time she got to the robe, "Star Trek" came back on, and took with it Chaim's attention.

She felt offended momentarily, but then she told herself, she was used to it by now. Something made her feel pensive, though, and she thought back in time. Perhaps she shouldn't have pushed the move from Lakewood after Suri was born, but she'd felt inadequate as a Kollel wife. Everyone had seemed able to handle living in a small apartment with no spending money. They all could do it better than she could. She'd wanted "a real life," with a big house and a husband who had a normal job. She hadn't foreseen that the TV would come with it.

It had started with a "closet TV" they took out only occasionally to watch reruns of "Quantum Leap." Once the genie got out of the bottle, however, there was no getting it back in. "Why watch in black and white when we can see it in color?" Chaim had asked her one day. Before she'd had a chance to think about it, the delivery men were bringing the new 26-inch TV into the den.

Miriam stared at it, shivers going down her spine. Did she really want this thing in her home? But Chaim couldn't wait to watch the 26-inch full-color picture. In what seemed moments he'd mastered all the functions on the remote control.

When Shabbos came, Miriam covered the new TV with a tapestry and placed a flowerpot on top. But she looked and looked at it, realizing that the effort was futile — it still looked like a TV covered with a tapestry and a flowerpot. She rationalized that the main Shabbos place was the dining room anyway, but she never felt comfortable about the thing sitting in the salon.

And now it had come to this dead end: Chaim sitting in a trance, gazing at the huge picture, ignoring her, ignoring life, ignoring the Torah he'd once cared about. But what could she do? "Don't stay up too late," she offered as she left the room, unnoticed, unheard. She went upstairs feeling a mixture of anger and guilt. Should she be mad at him or blame herself?

Chaim sat in front of the set, oblivious to all this, until the final credits appeared. He was just about to hit the Off button on the remote, while attempting to figure a way out of the recliner, when he gave a final glance at the TV, froze for a moment, and then smiled. Another episode of "Star Trek"! He sat back, and didn't get to bed until past one o'clock in the morning.

When Chaim looked at the bedside clock the next morning, right away he reproached himself. In what was becoming an unwanted habit, he'd once again overslept the minyan. He lifted his heavy frame out of bed, got dressed grumpily, found his tallis and tefillin, and went to his study. Sourly he thought, "This is a study? I never study any more. 'One-man synagogue' would be a better name for it."

He tried to daven, but found himself more concerned at this point with making his bus. After just twelve minutes he hurriedly peeled off his tallis and tefillin, took a glance at his watch — and sighed. Sure enough, he'd missed the bus again. He came into the kitchen and saw Miriam making sandwiches for the girls' lunch boxes. If she was surprised to see him, she didn't show it. But she was unusually curt. "Morning. Overslept again?"

He decided also to be brief. "Yep."

He joined Tehillah for a quick bowl of Trix, grabbed a few chocolate-chip cookies for the road, said a gruff "Bye," and squeezed into his Nissan Maxima.

When he'd left, Miriam stared at the door, then brought the dishtowel she was holding to her eyes and wiped them.

Once Chaim reached the Palisades Parkway he put the car on cruise control. Now, since he didn't have to concentrate much on driving, he began to think about the shows and movies he'd recently seen. "If the food on the Starship Enterprise is all computer-generated, does that mean it's kosher? ... How do you become a contestant on 'Survivor?' ... Wouldn't the 'Beverly Hillbillies' be a great reality series? ... If the professor is so smart, why didn't he just build a boat to get the castaways off of 'Gilligan's Island?' ... How come Lois Lane can't figure out that Clark Kent is Superman?"

Chaim's thoughts were flying through his head so quickly that he nearly drove through the tollbooth at the George Washington Bridge without paying. Once he got into Manhattan, he managed to find a garage to park his car. By the time he arrived in his office and turned on the computer, it was just nine.

The day was spent trying to write computer programs, and hoping the ones he'd written already worked. By ten-forty-five he was rubbing his eyes. He was tired of staring at a screen, after he'd done the same thing most of last night. And this was worse, because at least last night it had taken his mind off of things. So when he saw Dennis and Marv standing by the water cooler, he suddenly felt that he needed a break, and went over to have a drink.

Before he could say anything, Dennis said, "Chaim! Maybe you could remember this one. Who played Tarzan?"

Chaim replied immediately, "A lot of guys. The one you probably mean is Johnny Weismuller."

Marv smiled and said, "No, I mean the guy from that 60s TV series."

"Oh, Jim Hudson," Chaim replied instantly.

Dennis looked confused. "Henson? The Muppets guy?"

"Not Henson. Hudson. Like the river."

After a few minutes of talking about TV trivia, Chaim reluctantly went back to his computer. He yawned and stretched, trying to keep his mind focused. He started thinking about what he might be able to watch that night, but remembered he had to get his latest program debugged before he was free to think about other programs. The day went by slowly, the only highlights coming when Chaim astounded the secretaries with his encyclopedic knowledge of old TV shows.

Chaim stayed in the office until around six. He took the elevator down, stepped outside, and then saw the dusting of snow on the streets. He groaned. He never liked driving in snow, even a light covering. Shrugging, he bundled up his winter coat, placed his hat squarely on his head, and pulled on his gloves.

It was only two blocks to the parking lot. After he paid for the day he squeezed in behind the wheel (it was getting harder all the time) and drove off towards the George

Washington Bridge and the Palisades Parkway.

Chaim was feeling sleepy from spending all day at his computer after staying up so late the night before. By now he was wishing he could have taken a nap at some point in the day, but he could never have that luxury.

Snow or no snow, he managed to get across the upper level of the George Washington Bridge easily enough. Almost by rote he turned off and got on the Palisades north for the trip back to Monsey. He wasn't surprised at how few cars there were. He figured the weather must have scared everyone into staying home.

Chaim loved the Palisades Interstate Parkway. After all, it was largely responsible for transforming Monsey from a sleepy bungalow colony to a thriving metropolis of Torah. It was also among the most beautiful highways in America. "The only thing lacking," mused Chaim, "is neon signs, lights — something to give the road pizazz." In fact, the scanty highway lighting left the road dark at night. Very dark. "Boring," Chaim summed up in his mind. The high trees on either side even blocked out lights from the nearby towns.

The snow had stopped falling, leaving a light coating of ice on the highway. Unfortunately, instead of concentrating on safety, Chaim was once again indulging in his favorite pastime. "How come in Harry Potter children learn to be wizards, while on 'Bewitched' you were born that way? Why did they teach magic to children, who would just go and use it for dangerous things? Did Mary Poppins do magic? Is she doing an *aveirah*? If so, how could she be so nice and sweet? If not, how does she fly using an umbrella? How come Superman doesn't have to flap his arms to fly?"

Eight miles up the road, Jose Gonzales' vintage '73 Buick was just breathing its last. It died so quickly, Jose had no choice but to leave it in the right lane. Getting out, he cursed a bit, remembered his cell phone, then remembered it was cut off for non-payment. He cursed some more, then decided to try his luck at one of the homes he could make out through the thick trees. Maybe one of them would let him use the phone.

As Jose walked into the woods, Chaim was rapidly approaching — much too rapidly, considering that the darkness cut visibility down to a paltry ten feet. "The boxer in that movie the other night wasn't so realistic. Every punch he threw was a knockout punch, but that's a giveaway, no one could actually do that. Do they really ever 'throw in the towel'? How come boxers can't act, and actors can't box...?"

Just as he was reliving the final knockout punch the hero had given his opponent, the abandoned car came into view. With his mind still full of the powerful punch, Chaim's heart beat wildly as he saw the car in the right lane. He slammed on the brakes, but at fifty miles per hour on ice, his car went into a skid. The driver's-side door struck Jose's car with such force that Chaim's head banged against the window. He felt the searing pain, and then... darkness.

After a few moments, Chaim felt lighter than air. Maybe, he thought fuzzily, it was because he *was* lighter than air. He was looking down at the wreckage of his car — it was a lot worse than he'd expected. Ugh! He never could stand the gory parts in the movies, so he had a hard time looking down at that heavy-set guy in the driver's seat bleeding on the side of his face. It took a few moments to realize that he was that guy. It didn't seem to matter.

"Oh, so this must be an out-of-body experience," he thought calmly. He'd seen a documentary on late-night TV called "Life after Life," which dealt with experiences like this. He must be dead, that would explain the feeling of euphoria. So what came next? Wasn't there supposed to be a bright light or something? Almost on cue, Chaim saw the bright light coming from the sky. He began to follow it up.

He came to a room, where he saw his long-departed grandfather and great-uncle. They were dressed the way they did on Shabbos. There were also some of the Rabbanim from his yeshivah days who had since passed away, all dressed in their frock coats and homburg hats. He scanned the room and felt glad, seeing all these people whom he hadn't seen for years. In the corner, however, was one fellow who seemed out of place: a sloppy-looking, overweight man wearing only dungarees and a t-shirt. Then Chaim knew him: it was Bob Borden, who'd died of a heart attack a few months ago.

What was Borden doing here? Chaim couldn't understand it. He thought back through the eight years he'd had to work side-by-side with the man. It had been pretty bad. Chaim was overweight, but Borden was an avid beer drinker and weighed over three hundred pounds. His crude jokes and foul language would make a gas-station attendant blush, and he used both freely around the office.

Borden loved watching football on TV, and like Chaim he was a fan of the classics channel. TV trivia was practically the only thing Chaim had in common with Borden, but somehow that was enough reason for them to spend most of their lunch breaks speaking together. Borden was the only one Chaim knew who had an equally masterful memory of the reruns.

But he'd never liked Borden. He hadn't even really wanted any connection with him; only who else could he trade trivia with on that level? He'd never felt comfortable with Borden, and in fact, though he never said so publicly, for at least a few moments Chaim was relieved when he heard about Borden's fatal heart attack at the age of 54. So what was he seeing now? Was his link with this foul-mouthed lowlife going to extend even into the World of Truth?

Suddenly Chaim heard a siren, then felt his body being carried into an ambulance. A few words penetrated his daze: "He's coming around!" He tried to move his body, but it felt twisted like a twizzler, and he felt a sharp pain on the side of his face.

He thought, "What happened? Which world am I in now? Was I just in a car accident? Did I go to the next world for a few moments? Was it all a dream?"

Chaim was in a daze when they got to Englewood Hospital. He was immediately sent to the Intensive Care Unit, where they stitched his face up, fitted a support frame over his ribcage, and hooked him to an ECG to monitor his heartbeat.

A few hours later he was allotted a bed in a regular ward. By now he just felt groggy. His face was stiff, covered with bandages, and his ribcage hurt every time he breathed.

Suddenly he looked up and saw a doctor holding a clipboard, standing in front of his bed. The doctor looked closely at Chaim for a few moments, then asked, "Can you hear me?"

Chaim nodded. He managed to ask, "Where am I?"

"You're in Englewood Hospital. You do know you were in a car accident, don't you?"

Chaim simply said, "Yes."

"The main damage was to your face and the ribcage. You gave the ambulance personnel a real scare when your heartbeat stopped for a few minutes, probably from the shock of the crash. The CPR in the ambulance saved you."

After the doctor left, Chaim managed to call Miriam and tell her what had happened. Within forty minutes she was by his bedside. She tried to reassure Chaim that everything would be all right, but he could tell right away that she didn't sound convinced. Why was her voice trembling? After a few minutes she had to excuse herself, and left the room. Chaim couldn't figure out why she was acting this way. Did she blame herself in some way for the accident? When she came back, Chaim could tell that she had washed her face. She'd been crying. He didn't know why, didn't know even how to ask her why. Since this wasn't *The X-Men*, he couldn't hear her thinking, "I encouraged him to leave learning and go to work full-time, and now this is how it ends."

Chaim wanted to tell his wife about what he'd seen during those strange few minutes, but once again he couldn't think how to bring up the subject. Anyway, she didn't seem to be in any shape to listen. Instead he said, "Please tell Rabbi Goodman what's happened. And next time you come, can you bring me something?"

Miriam said, "Sure, what?" Inwardly, she was hoping he wouldn't ask her to buy a portable DVD player.

"Bring me a tape deck, please, and some Torah tapes."

What was this? Miriam could hardly believe her ears. "It must be from the traumatic experience," she thought. All the same, for the first time that evening she smiled.

Rabbi Goodman came to visit the next day. After some small talk, Chaim couldn't hold himself back. He had to tell someone who might understand. He said hesitatingly, "Um, I've had this strange experience."

Rabbi Goodman asked, "A strange experience? What kind?"

"You're probably not going to believe this one," Chaim said softly.

Rabbi Goodman waved his hand, "Try me. My students tell me a lot of crazy stories."

Chaim paused for a moment, and in his most serious voice he said firmly, "I think that I went briefly to the next world."

After a moment of silence, Rabbi Goodman replied steadily, "All right, could you tell me about it?"

Chaim took a deep breath. "Right after the accident, I

temporarily lost consciousness. I think I made a short visit to heaven. Once they gave me CPR in the ambulance, it revived me, and I was back in this world."

Through his bandages, Chaim studied Rabbi Goodman's features. When he saw that Rabbi Goodman was listening intently and didn't shrug the incident aside as a strange dream, he felt a surge of relief.

"Describe everything to me," Rabbi Goodman offered.

Chaim told him all about floating above the crash site, seeing his mangled body, the feeling of euphoria, the bright light, and the room where he saw his departed loved ones — and Bob Borden.

Rabbi Goodman nodded his head and said, "I've read some accounts of the NDE — near-death experience — and this all fits in."

Chaim smiled and asked excitedly, "It does?"

"Yes," Rabbi Goodman replied. He was about to add, "It's a shame you weren't allowed to see a bit more," but caught himself. Wishing that someone could have stayed dead longer is not something you tell a hospital patient. Instead he added, "It also fits into what Chazal say about the world to come."

Chaim was fascinated. "How so?"

"Let me ask you something. Did you ever wonder why Hashem gave you your five senses?"

Chaim thought that one was easy. "So I could perceive the world around me," he answered.

"But from what you've just told me, you could see without your eyes and hear without your ears!"

Chaim lay there dumbfounded. It seemed a ridiculous

question, but now he had to ask it. "Then why do we have senses?"

Rabbi Goodman explained, "The senses limit what the mind takes in, so it can function in this world. Once the mind is free from the body, everything we looked at and saw in our life is revealed. All the things you ever thought and dealt with come together and make up your experience in the next world."

Chaim was in shock. He'd never thought about it that way. He meekly asked, "How do we know this?"

"I saw it once in a commentary on Pirkei Avos on the *mishnah*, 'Look into three things and you won't end up sinning: an eye that sees, an ear that hears, and all your deeds written in the book.' Didn't you ever wonder why it doesn't say 'a hand that writes all your deeds in the book'? The answer is that your actions do the writing all by themselves. What you do and what you think make up your life in the next world."

Chaim felt relief that here was someone who could relate to his experience; but then his heart began to race when he realized what he'd just heard. Whatever his mind dwelled on in this world would make up his life in the world to come! Now something really bothered him. Actually, it was the same thing that had made him speak with the Rabbi in the first place.

"Why do you think that guy Borden was with my relatives?"

"I don't have the secrets of the next world at my disposal. But perhaps you yourself can tell me. How did you come to know him?"

Chaim told about the eight unhappy years that they were forced to work together. Rabbi Goodman stared at Chaim with his piercing brown eyes. "You say that the only thing you had in common with this Borden fellow was TV, is that right?"

"Right. That's absolutely the only thing we had in common."

"So perhaps since this thing gave you a sort of kinship, he was permitted to be in your portion."

"Kinship? With *him*?"

"Well, yes. While you were laughing and enjoying reruns in your house, he was laughing and enjoying the same programs in his house. And then you would talk over these shows at length the next day. So your minds were frequently occupied with the very same things. Once both your minds were released from the body, you and he entered a world that shared some of its aspects."

The words brought chills down Chaim's spine. Who knew how much time he'd have to spend with Borden in the next world? The thought of sharing any time at all was making him sick.

Rabbi Goodman noticed the hurt look on his *talmid's* bandaged face. He gently offered, "It's never too late, Chaim. Get rid of that TV now, and use your mind for greater purposes, ones that I know you have the potential for."

Chaim looked at the hospital ceiling for a few moments.

The nurse abruptly walked in and told Rabbi Goodman that visiting hours were over. Rabbi Goodman shook

Chaim's hand and said, "I'll try to visit again sometime this week. What's your name again?"

Chaim said, "Chaim ben Rivkah." After Rabbi Goodman turned to the door, he added, "Thanks for coming."

That evening Miriam came with a large Wesley Kosher bag in one hand and two envelopes in the other. She smiled when she saw that her husband seemed a bit better. "I borrowed these tapes from the *gemach,* and here's a tape deck." Chaim could tell that there was something else, something large, in the bag.

"What else is in there?" he asked.

She said, "I thought you might also want this." She held up an ArtScroll Gemara, *Masechta Sanhedrin.* "I asked around, and that's what the Daf Yomi's on now."

Chaim smiled through his bandages. "How did you know? You're so thoughtful. It's just what I wanted."

Miriam wasn't sure that was Chaim behind those bandages. It was quite some time since she'd heard a compliment.

"What's with the envelopes?" he asked.

"Oh, they gave me them downstairs. One is to order a phone, the other is for a TV. I told them you'd probably want both."

Chaim countered, "Um, let's skip the TV."

Now Miriam couldn't believe what she was hearing. She knew her husband was in the hospital, but now she was worried that maybe he had some undetected brain damage. Chaim, however, went right on. "Listen, I want you to take that money for the TV rental and get the phone hooked up to Dial-a-Daf."

"Why don't you want the TV?" Miriam asked, bewildered.

"Let's just say I didn't like the coming attractions."

Well Adjusted

"What's going on here?" Michael Plotsky yelled, as he turned a bright shade of red. "You just sent that order now? I promised him it would be there on the twelfth!"

Mrs. Silverstein was shaking. If she didn't need the job so badly, she wouldn't mind getting fired. Anything to escape from this tyrant. Drawing a deep breath, she managed to stammer, "I'm so sorry, sir, but you didn't tell me that. I thought...."

"You're not supposed to think," Michael barked. "You're supposed to do as you're told. You've really messed things up — again!"

He grumbled all the way to his office, slamming the door behind him. Before he could pick up the phone to sort out the latest crisis, he suddenly felt pains in his stomach. He looked at the clock. It was time to take his ulcer medicine. His doctor had warned him not to get excited like this, but what was he supposed to do, surrounded with incompetents like this?... He swiveled his chair around and got a bottle of Poland Spring water from the small refrigerator in the corner. After downing two pills he picked up the phone, still grumbling.

Talking to Abrams' secretary, he did his best to offer apologies for the delayed shipment. Unfortunately, he was still fuming, so he didn't sound very sweet, or even apologetic. The secretary ended up telling him in a crisp, business-like voice that Mr. Abrams wasn't in right now, and he would get back to him in a day or two.

By mid-afternoon Plotsky had calmed down somewhat. Not that he was ever very calm. In fact, when he heard Mrs. Silverstein on the intercom he just barked, "What do you want this time?"

Mrs. Silverstein said, "A Mr. Simchah Rothstein is here to see you."

"Who?"

"The name he gave was Simchah Rothstein."

"Ask him what in blazes he wants. If he's here to sell me something, get rid of him."

After a few moments Mrs. Silverstein answered, "He says he's a fundraiser, and that he has an appointment for three o'clock."

"Oh." Michael quickly checked his palm pilot and saw that a fundraiser was indeed scheduled. "Oh, yeah. Tell him to hold his horses. I'll get to him when I can spare a few moments." Twenty minutes later he told Mrs. Silverstein to let "that guy" in.

Simchah Rothstein approached the desk and saw Michael sitting there in his expensive suit. He seemed to have a tired and worried look about him, but he shook Simchah's hand firmly and asked him brusquely, "Which organization do you represent?"

Simchah handed Mr. Plotsky his card, and told him in broken English all about the *cheder* he'd founded. He was about to mention how they emphasized *middos* and the study of VaYikra, when Michael suddenly held up his hand. Simchah stopped in mid-word.

Michael squinted and asked, "Where is this *cheder*?"

Simchah stammered, "Near the Bokharan Quarter, not

far from Geulah."

"I thought so. I'm afraid I won't be able to help you."

Simchah had been told to expect this response, only he was hoping in the back of his mind that maybe this time would be different. Successfully hiding his disappointment, he shook Mr. Plotsky's hand once more, and looking at the floor, walked out.

As soon as he set foot out of the office, Simchah's face fell. Mrs. Silverstein noticed how upset he was and asked sympathetically, "Get anything?"

Simchah said, "No."

"You shouldn't feel bad. Mr. Plotsky doesn't usually support institutions in Eretz Yisrael."

Simchah swallowed hard. "Why not?"

"Oh, he feels he can't monitor the funds as well as he'd like to. He's had some occasions where he felt he may have been ripped off by fraudulent institutions. He generally supports only places that are well known, or if he personally knows the directors."

Once he was certain another disappointed collector had left, Michael walked out of his office. He said accusingly, "I'm sick of these guys coming from who-knows-where to beg from me. From now on, find out where they're from, and if it's Israel, tell them to get lost."

The rest of the day passed without incident, except for when he chewed out Mrs. Silverstein for buying the wrong brand of coffee ("I specifically told you I wanted decaf", only he hadn't). And there was the accusation, later on, that she was being careless with his money by keeping the air conditioner on too high.

Around seven that evening Michael left the office. As usual, after work he felt drained, hungry and tired. The heat didn't help. With his wife and children at the bungalow colony for the summer, he usually ate supper at the Rose Palace catering hall. Somehow he managed to make his way up the stairs and find the buffet. He was so tired.

Hardly anyone was there at this late hour. Michael had just sat down, at a table by himself, when from the corner of his eye he saw someone he knew come in. He dismissed the thought, but then he took another look, and realized it was his nephew Avrumi. He'd always liked Avrumi. The thought slipped through his mind momentarily that Avrumi was almost the only human being that he did like. Hurriedly brushing the thought aside he called out, "Avrumi? Is that you?"

Avrumi slowly approached his uncle, a plastic supermarket shopping bag in one hand. *"Shalom aleichem,"* said Avrumi in his rapid mumble.

"Aleichem shalom. What brings you here from the mountains?"

"My old roommate at Lakewood, Yonah Peretz, is making a bris tomorrow. Also, my mother's not too happy with the selection at the sefarim store in the mountains, so I picked up the latest Targum release for her."

Plotsky had to listen carefully. His nephew had a habit of talking twice as fast and twice as soft as most people. You had to have some experience to understand him. But Plotsky was always interested in what Avrumi had to say; the effort to understand was never a bother.

Avrumi was asking, "How's the food here?" For a moment his uncle frowned at the question. Avrumi gave a quick smirk.

Michael shrugged and said, "Let's just say I like home cooking anywhere. It's really not so bad. It's a mitzvah for the Agudah to arrange these meals for us men while our families are away."

Avrumi smiled, and lifted the bag he was carrying. "Maybe this will make it a little tastier," he said as he pulled out of the bag a two-liter Pepsi bottle filled with water. "It's from the well at the bungalow colony. I filled it for you right after Shabbos."

Michael's face lit up. "*Yishar koach!* Just at the right time. I was getting really tired of that Poland Spring stuff. It's just not real."

"What? You don't like the bottled water? I thought that's all you drank," Avrumi said, with surprise in his voice.

Michael answered, "Well, even grocery-store water is better than tap water. Yuck! I don't know how anybody can drink that stuff. But the bottled water isn't real either: it's just tap water that's been filtered, and then treated with chemicals so it tastes a little better. Then they put it in these plastic bottles that sit in the sun on a supermarket shelf for months. I can taste the plastic in the water. There's nothing on earth even half as good as real, pure well water."

Michael stopped a moment and thought. When he had heard there was a real well, complete with an old-fashioned red pump, at Avrumi's bungalow colony, his first impulse was to sell his place in town and move out there. His wife Aidel quickly nixed that idea. "We've been here for over fifteen years," she told him, "and I'm not moving just so you can be closer to your water." With no alternative, Michael often visited Avrumi's bungalow colony, just so he could stock up on the sweet, pure well water.

Now Avrumi had brought him some, right in the middle of this hot, thirsty summer. Michael quickly poured himself a cup, said the *berachah,* and took a drink.

"Would you like some?" he asked Avrumi.

Avrumi said, "No, thanks. I've got to get to the sefarim store before they close. I've got to run, take care, Uncle."

Michael exclaimed, "Shalom, and thanks again for the water!"

Avrumi shambled out while Michael sat back and savored another cup. Suddenly he felt his head swirling. At the same time his insides felt as if they were doing somersaults. He thought for a moment that it had something to do with his ulcer, but then, just as suddenly, the feelings stopped.

"That was weird," he thought. He sat back for a few moments and got his bearings. Everything seemed to be okay. He took a few more sips, and realized that his mind felt fresh and invigorated. He had a sudden clarity he'd never experienced before in his life. He sat there motionless for a few moments, trying to take in what had just happened. He took a few deep breaths, and felt great. It was as if his body was brand new.

He slowly rose, and even though it was an hour before his Daf Yomi *shiur* he went to the Beis Midrash.

During the *shiur* Rabbi Lerer noticed several changes in Michael. To begin with, he didn't fall asleep as he usually did. Even more unusual, he asked several penetrating questions and seemed really interested in getting *peshat*.

Michael davened Maariv that night as if it was Yom Kippur. After waiting for him to finish, his neighbor Feivush proposed to walk home with Michael as they usually did.

"No thanks," Michael said kindly. "I want to review the *daf*, and then — I think I need to do some accounts. Internal ones, *cheshbon hanefesh*."

Feivush looked at Michael strangely. "Everything okay? What's got into you?"

"What got into me? Don't you realize we're all going to die one day? What good is our money when we can't take it with us? I used to think a person can't have too much money, but that's not true. A person can't have too many mitzvos! You only go around once in life, so you've got to grab all you can in the short time we're in this world."

Feivush looked at Michael, wondering if he'd gone crazy. What was going on here? Why was he talking this way? "I hope he's all right" was all he managed to say, under his breath, as he walked out the door.

The next day Rabbi Lerer was shocked to find Michael in shul twenty minutes before davening, already in his *tallis* and *tefillin*. He noticed Michael was saying *Korbanos*. That had never happened before. "He usually makes it just in time for *Barchu*," thought the Rabbi. "Well! I hope others use him for an example."

Later that morning Mrs. Silverstein walked trembling up the corridor to the office. She was near the end of her endurance, and knew it. She'd considered phoning in sick that morning, but if she did she'd probably be fired. As she knocked on the door, she briefly noticed that her fingernails were chewed down to the quick. They'd been like that ever since she took this job.

After Michael said, "Come in," Mrs. Silverstein entered, shaking worse than ever. The first thing she noticed was a change in her boss' demeanor. He looked refreshed, as if he'd just got back from vacation. That sight alone put her somewhat at ease, and with sudden confidence she managed to say, "While you were out yesterday, sir, Mr. Abrams called. He said that since we were late shipping that order, they'll have to re-examine their account with us. I'm very sorry, sir." She braced herself for the explosion.

But, to her astonishment, Mr. Plotsky didn't erupt. He didn't even raise his voice. What was even more shocking, she saw him do something he rarely did in the office — he smiled. "So what? All that we're supposed to earn is decreed on Rosh Hashanah. Even if we lose the account, we'll get another one to replace it. And anyway, it's my fault. I never gave you a final shipping date for that order."

Mrs. Silverstein couldn't believe her ears! Was this the same Michael Plotsky she had worked for the past five months, whom some of the non-Jewish staff referred to as a "slave driver, a tyrant, a dictator"? The same Michael Plotsky who was always running Help Wanted ads, since no worker could stand him too long? She'd been warned before she took this job that it came with the risk of high pressure, from a boss with an ulcer and even higher blood pressure. It'd been true, too, and worse.

She'd never heard him speak like this. He seemed suddenly so well adjusted.

The shocks weren't over, either. Plotsky went right on, and softly suggested, "You know, I just had an idea. What if we offered Torah *shiurim* during the lunch break? I've heard that it's done in several other businesses. Could you please look into it for us?"

Mrs. Silverstein stood there, unable to move or speak. A stunned smile gradually spread across her face, and dizzily she thought, "Since it's a day for miracles, why not try my luck?" Out loud she said tremulously, "Well, my husband is a Rebbe, and he's looking for some extra income during the summer."

"Fine, have him call me tomorrow to set up the interview. I'm prepared to offer him liberal terms."

Mrs. Silverstein left the inner office beaming, and scratching her head.

Once she was gone, Michael got his wife on the phone. He said cheerily, "Hi, honey. How're things upstate?"

"It's a little cramped. When are we doing that expansion?"

"I don't think we need it."

She quickly answered, "That's what you always say, but I'm feeling claustrophobic in this bungalow."

Michael said, "I think we should sell it."

"I told you a thousand times, I like it here in Meadow Valley," she rapidly said. "I'm not moving to Greenlawn bungalows just so you can be near your well."

Michael calmly responded, "I didn't have that in mind."

"Then what did you have in mind?" she said with a note of confusion.

In his most serious voice Michael said, "I've had a great idea. Let's move to Israel."

Mrs. Plotsky laughed. "Very funny."

He ignored that comment and continued. "I've figured it all out," he said. "We can sell the Meadow Valley bungalow and the house in Brooklyn, and buy a villa in Beit Shemesh. I can sit and learn for a few years."

His wife suddenly stopped laughing. He couldn't be serious, could he? Nah! She decided to play along for a moment. "If we're going already, I want to live in the Old City near the Kotel."

Michael said excitedly, "The Kotel? That's a great idea! I was thinking more along the lines of Beit Shemesh, but if it'll make you happy, I'll go for the Old City."

Was he taking her seriously? This joke had gone on long enough. "C'mon, you're kidding, right?"

"Would I kid about this? I mean it," Michael firmly said.

Mrs. Plotsky shifted uneasily in her seat. He really did sound serious.

"Have you forgotten that you've never been to Israel?"

"Then it's about time I go."

"Just like that?"

"I suppose a pilot trip might be a good idea."

Finally, she shrieked. "Are you serious? Me? Live in Israel? In a tiny apartment?"

Michael quickly replied, "It won't be much different than the bungalow you're in now, and every summer you seem to manage just fine!"

"You can't be serious!" she said, with desperation in her voice.

Michael realized that perhaps this was a bit too abrupt. "I know this may seem too much for you," he said sympathetically, "we'll talk about it when I come up for Shabbos."

Mrs. Plotsky hung up the phone, bewildered. "What's gotten into him?" she thought.

Michael sat back in his chair. For once, he started cleaning his desk himself. As he was rummaging through, he came across Simchah Rothstein's card. Without a second thought, he quickly wrote out a sizable check and sent it off.

After stepping out for Minchah, for a change he washed his hands, and then spent about half an hour davening. Then, since he was in the Beis Midrash already, he decided he might as well stay there a while. Work just didn't seem as important as it always had. It could stand a bit of delay.

After about a half an hour, however, he began to have trouble concentrating. "What am I doing here?" he thought to himself irritably. "Am I going to spend all day learning?" Instinctively he shut his Gemara and decided it was time to get something to eat.

Since it was only six o'clock — earlier than he usually left the office — when he made his way to the Rose Palace some of the other members of his shul were there as well. He got his meal, and put his tray down in an open spot at a table where some of his friends were eating. Going over to the communal fridge, he got out his precious bottle of real well water and poured himself a cup. After a few bites and a sip he motioned to the bottle and said to Feivush, "You want to try something really good?"

Feivush's eyes lit up. "What is it?"

"Real well water from my nephew's bungalow colony."

"Sure, I'll try some."

Feivush drank a few sips, and suddenly he felt his head spinning. He didn't know what was happening. As Plotsky had, he felt his insides turning inside out. He was about to scream when, just as suddenly, it stopped.

"Real well water?" Shayah asked. "Can I have some?"

Right after Shayah drank a cup, Michael noticed his friend holding his head and looking odd. For a moment he seemed as if he might fall off his chair. Michael was about to ask if he was okay, but then Shayah shook off whatever it was and seemed normal again. Actually, Michael was feeling a bit peculiar too. "Why did I leave the Beis Midrash so soon today?" he kept thinking. "What came over me?"

All three drank a few more cups of the water with their dinner, and soon the bottle was empty.

Feivush sat back in his chair. He suddenly felt different. "What am I doing here? Who am I?" he wondered. "I'm a diamond dealer, and that's a way to make a living, but should it be *who I am?* What do I do all day? Make money. But I don't need any more money, I have enough; so why am I doing this? I live in Boro Park, but what good is my fancy house if I'm going to leave this world in a few years?

Anyway, I work so late that I'm hardly ever at home. We just put in that fancy kitchen and now my wife works so late that most of the time we have to order take-out! I'm already 52; most people don't make it past eighty. What am I doing to myself?"

Shayah was thinking similar thoughts. "My accounting firm has thirty employees. They don't really need me to be there all day.... My house must be worth around $750,000. I could sell it, and buy a smaller one and use the balance to support *yeshivos* and *chadarim*. Better yet, I could go to Eretz Yisrael and sit and learn; then I'd be making a mitzvah out of every moment. Sure, it would work... I'd make a monthly visit over here to supervise the business, at my age that would be enough to keep me comfortable. The rest of the time is for my *neshamah*.

"A man never has too many mitzvos. You can't take certificates of deposit or college degrees with you to the next world, only Torah and mitzvos. So why am I spending all day doing something that won't last?"

After they ate, all three got up to wash *mayim acharonim*, and for the first time they remembered not to speak after they washed. They *bentsched* together as if it was the last mitzvah they would do in this world. Then, forgetting whatever they had planned to do that evening, they ran together to the Beis Midrash.

The next morning all three arrived for Shacharis early, and after a quick breakfast and an hour at the office, went back to the shul to learn together. Yitzhak Saver stopped in briefly at ten-thirty that morning to pick up a sefer he'd forgotten, and saw the trio there. When he came later on in the afternoon to daven Minchah, he was shocked to see the three of them back again in their seats. What was going on here? "You guys on a seminar or something?" he asked.

"Why do you say that?" asked Feivush.

"This morning, I stopped in for a second and I saw you guys here. Now you're here again. Are you spending all day here?"

Feivush said, "If only we could! But you have to give your *parnassah* at any rate an hour in the morning and an hour in the afternoon, even at our age. What's so odd if we spend the rest of our time learning? Shouldn't everyone? We're only passing through this world."

Yitzhak looked dumbfounded, so Feivush went on: "Let's say you're given ten minutes in a supermarket, and all you can grab you can keep. Would you grab the paper towels or the steaks? We've just realized that we're only in this world for a short time, and we've got to grab all the steaks — the mitzvos — that we can."

Shayah added, "Suppose you were on a talent show. Wouldn't you prepare and rehearse, and when you get on stage, give your best performance? Pretty soon we're all going Upstairs, so we'd better get prepared, and put on the best show possible."

Yitzhak suddenly got to thinking. If these three high-powered shul members should suddenly take time out of their day to sit and learn, why shouldn't he?

Next day, the four were in shul early, then after davening settled down to learn. Rabbi Lerer was impressed with the sudden arousal in some members of his congregation. He wanted to know who organized this sudden outpouring, and approached Michael, who simply told him, "We don't have many years left, and we have to grab every mitzvah we can. How can I waste my time sleeping?" After a brief pause, he added, "We've been meaning to ask you, do you think you could start a *shiur* for us at 5:30 tomorrow morning?"

That morning Michael was in the middle of what he'd started calling his "office hour" when he got a shock: his wife Aidel walked in. With a smile he said, "Honey! What brings you here? You almost never come in from the mountains."

She said, "I have an appointment for you."

"For me? Where?"

"At the doctor's. You're acting weird, and I want to be sure everything is all right."

A cab ride later, they were sitting in the doctor's office.

"All this is really unnecessary, " Michael pronounced.

"They told me you spent most of the day in the Beis Midrash, took almost an hour to daven Minchah, you're planning on hiring a Rav to say *shiur* in the office, and gave a huge donation to a charity, in Israel yet. Something's going on with you."

Michael said calmly, "I don't have much time left."

Aidel gasped. "Do you have some awful disease you're not telling me about?"

"No."

"Then why do you keep saying you don't have much time left? This is the third time you've used that phrase.

The doctor will prove to you that you're fine, or if there's something wrong we can treat it, and if not, maybe he could explain your strange behavior."

After the check-up Dr. Wagner said, "He's in perfect health. Even his ulcer is gone, all of a sudden, and his blood pressure is normal. What'd you do, Michael?"

Michael just lifted his eyes towards heaven.

Feivush also had to see a doctor that day, but his was a more serious ailment. He hadn't told anyone yet, but a recent biopsy had shown lung cancer. His pack-a-day habit was catching up with him. He was getting treatment now, and the doctor had just ordered some tests to see how the treatment was going.

Feivush finished at the lab and sat down to await the results. When the nurse called him in, he found his doctor staring at the forms in shock. "These must be from the wrong patient. There's no sign of cancer anywhere!" He rechecked the name and the code on the tests. Sure enough, it was Feivush. The doctor looked up and half-shouted, "I've heard of spontaneous remission, but never in lung cancer before. These lungs look like you haven't smoked in years!"

"Well, I did quit. " Feivush said.

"When?" the doctor asked.

"Yesterday."

Doctor Wagner's eyes almost fell out of his head. "Yesterday? It takes years off of cigarettes before the lungs clean out like this! I can't understand what has happened, but it's a miracle, Feivush. You are a very lucky man."

At five-thirty the next morning, Rabbi Lerer was counting on the foursome to come to the *shiur*. Perhaps they would have talked a few others into trying it out. He was very surprised when the only one who showed up was Yitzhak Saver. Rabbi Lerer smiled crookedly, and gave the *shiur* nonetheless. He looked at the door a few times, wondering if any other of the four would have the decency of showing up for what he'd requested.

While Yitzhak put on his tefillin and said *Korbanos*, Rabbi Lerer waited for Feivush, Shayah, or Michael to come in. Two didn't show up at all, and Michael Plotsky barged in, according to his old custom, two minutes before *Barchu*.

At 9:30, Mrs. Silverstein knocked on the door of Michael's inner office. Plotsky grunted, "Come in."

Mrs. Silverstein smiled and said, "I spoke to my husband and he's interested in the *shiurim*. When should I schedule the interview?"

Michael rudely growled, "Interview? For what, if I may ask?"

"Uh-oh," she thought, already starting to tremble. "I don't like that tone." She found her voice, and said, "For the *shiurim* you asked me to arrange for lunch break."

Plotsky's forehead wrinkled. He vaguely remembered something. It was all like a dream. Certainly not a reality. He wasn't interested. "Well," he snarled, "after that order you messed up, I don't know if we'll have the budget for such luxuries in this office."

Mrs. Silverstein's face darkened, but she kept silent. She knew better than to say anything. Plotsky, meanwhile, ranted on. "Perhaps you can come up with some ways to earn some money around here, instead of wasting it. And turn that air-conditioner higher. I'm sweating in here. Whoever told you to lower it?"

That night, before Maariv, when Rabbi Lerer saw Michael he walked up to him and asked, "What happened to you this morning? I thought you were one of the people who asked for the *shiur.*"

Michael froze for a moment, searching for words. Finally he blurted out, "Yeah, I don't know what came over me the last day or two. I haven't been myself. Right when all this was happening, I found out my ulcer's gone, and my blood pressure suddenly became normal. It's like I'm not myself any more." Rabbi Lerer stood open-mouthed while Michael walked away.

After Maariv Feivush approached Rabbi Lerer. Before he got a chance to ask him anything, Rabbi Lerer jumped in and asked, "What happened with the morning *shiur?*"

Feivush blushed for a moment, then said, "Well, I was really motivated yesterday, but it just sort of wore off. I kinda overslept davening this morning. Oh, and I wanted to ask you, do I have to *bentsch gomel?*"

"*Bentsch gomel?* For what?" the Rabbi asked curiously.

"Well, I had this problem with lung cancer. The doctor said my lungs were clogged with soot. He said it was one of the worst cases he'd ever seen. When I went back today for the check-up, my lungs were suddenly all clean. The doctor said it was a miracle."

Rabbi Lerer froze. What was going on here? Four of his shul members suddenly act like *tzaddikim?* Two of them suddenly have their illnesses healed? Rabbi Lerer didn't answer Feivush's question. Instead he said, "Could you and Michael please come to my study? I'd like to get to the bottom of this."

A few minutes later they were both sitting facing the Rabbi, who was seated at his desk. Rabbi Lerer got right to the point. "You were both suddenly cured, is that right?"

They looked at each other. "Yep."

Rabbi Lerer asked, "Did either of you get a *berachah,* or get a *kameia* to wear?"

Feivush shook his head. "The doctor asked me the same thing. I told him the only healthy thing I've had in the past few days was some well water."

The Rabbi's forehead wrinkled. "Well water? From where?"

Michael jumped in, "My sister's bungalow colony. There's nothing special in that water, I've been drinking it for years and nothing like this ever happened to me before."

Rabbi Lerer thought hard. There was only this one line to follow, so he would. He turned toward Michael. "How did you get this water?"

"My nephew brought it to me."

Rabbi Lerer stared at Michael for a moment, and asked, "Did he say when he took it from the well?"

Michael stared at the ceiling for a moment. "He said he took it on Motzaei Shabbos." At that Rabbi Lerer's eyes opened wide. He asked, trying not to sound hysterical, "Do you have any more of this water? Even a few drops? The bottle?"

Michael couldn't understand what was so exciting about some well water.

"We finished the water, and I threw the bottle out. If you want me to, I'll have him bring some more."

"No, I don't think that will be necessary," the Rabbi said with disappointment. "I think I can explain what's going on here. Only the water from the *be'er shel Miriam* could do this."

Feivush and Michael looked at each other. They'd drunk water from Miriam's Well? Could it be possible? Feivush asked, his voice quivering, "It's still around today, that well?"

Rabbi Lerer said, "Oh yes. Only five hundred years ago the Ari took his *talmid*, R. Chaim Vital, out on a boat to a spot in the Kinneret. He gave him a drink from that particular spot, explaining that it was not ordinary water. Miriam's Well sat in this location all week long, mingling its water with that of the Kinneret. The same well the Children of Israel drank from during their forty years in the desert is still with us today. R. Chaim Vital reported that after drinking the water of Miriam's well his mind was open to understand the secrets of Torah as he never could before."

Michael blustered, "But this water's from upstate, not the Kinneret!"

Rabbi Lerer lifted his hand, got up, and took from his bookshelf the third volume of the Mishnah Berurah. He found the page he was looking for, then said, "I'm paraphrasing the Rama in *Orach Chaim,* סימן רצ"ט סעיף י: 'Some people have the custom to drink water from a well every Motzaei Shabbos, because the water of Miriam's Well travels to every well in the world on Motzaei Shabbos, and if someone should drink from that water he will be cured immediately from all his ailments.'"

Rabbi Lerer closed the sefer, gave it a kiss, and put it on his desk. Both Michael and Feivush had turned white. Rabbi Lerer continued calmly, "The Rambam says that bad *middos* are also a *machalah,* a disease of the soul that needs to be cured. That explains why the four of you suddenly wanted to learn and daven more: you wanted more *kedushah* in your lives. That would also be why you wanted to move to *Eretz HaKodesh.*"

Michael's teeth chattered. He had drunk from Miriam's Well? He stammered, "Does that mean I'm cured for life?"

"The bodily diseases that you had have been cured, but that doesn't mean that your good health is guaranteed from now on. For example, your ulcer and high blood pressure can easily return if you act the way you did before you were healed."

"Why didn't the clarity and the drive to learn last?" questioned Feivush.

Rabbi Lerer answered, "Ah, because bad *middos* are not a bodily disease, and can't be cured by any medicine. Even Miriam's Well can only alleviate them for a moment; after that it all depends on the choices you make.

"You can't become a *tzaddik* simply by drinking some water; you have to work hard and practice behaving the right way. Remember, Dasan and Aviram, and the *erev rav* too, drank from Miriam's Well along with everyone else. Changing yourself takes hard work and making the right choices, again and again."

The men looked perplexed, so Rabbi Lerer explained further. "Look, in the sixties there was a theory about a method called 'sleep learning.' You would wear special headphones when you went to bed for the night, and put on a tape of a lecture. The theory was that the subconscious mind would understand the tape while you slept. You'd wake up the next day and know things you didn't know before."

Rabbi Lerer paused momentarily, then continued.

"There's only one problem. It didn't work, not one bit. The easy ways never work. It takes conscious effort to learn anything, and it's the same with *middos*. You can't just drink some water and automatically you're a *tzaddik*. The water of Miriam's Well opens up the mind, but more mundane thoughts can close it just as quickly. Think of medicine: it can cure a disease, but if a person plays in the snow without his coat he'll get sick again."

"I don't understand," protested Michael. "If all this was only temporary, what about Yitzhak? He's still out there learning, and I heard he's still planning on moving to Israel."

Rabbi Lerer sat there silently with a shocked expression. "Wasn't he with you when you drank from the bottle?"

Michael shook his head, "Shayah had some with us, but Yitzhak wasn't there."

Now Rabbi Lerer was really confused. Could there be some more water from Miriam's Well around? "Could he possibly have drunk from it without you knowing?"

Michael thought for a second, then answered, "I suppose it's possible. It was in an ordinary Pepsi bottle, and I kept it overnight in the communal fridge."

All the Rabbi said was, "Let's see if Shayah or Yitzhak is still here."

Yitzhak was learning *mishnayos* in the now-empty Beis Midrash. When he saw the Rabbi approaching, he quickly stood up. Rabbi Lerer asked him to step into his study for a moment.

When Yitzhak walked in, he saw Michael and Feivush sitting there. Right away he said "Hey, guys, where were you this morning? It was a good *shiur,* even if I was the only one there. Rabbi, you making sure these guys show up from now on?"

Rabbi Lerer said, "Um, it looks as if the *shiur* may just be a *chavrusa,* but that's fine with me."

"Oh, okay. Anyway, it won't be for too long. I heard what you guys were saying about moving to Eretz Yisrael, and having to grab every mitzvah you can while you're in this world. It got under my skin, you know, so I spoke to my wife, and she's really excited about it."

Michael asked, "You're really planning on moving to Israel?"

"We've been thinking about it for years, but hearing you guys talk the way you did made up my mind. My wife is planning on cutting her stay in the bungalow short this year, so we can leave by August and get the kids to school in time in Eretz Yisrael."

"Aren't you worried about *parnassah?*" asked Rabbi Lerer.

"Well, we have some saved up, and then I guess I'll look for something, like everyone else."

"But aren't you worried with the situation there now?"

"Do I have a choice? It's not safe anywhere in the world nowadays. And I've always wanted do this. Then, last night, I saw all you guys sitting and learning and talking about moving and all, and I just couldn't figure out what in blazes I was doing here in Brooklyn."

Rabbi Lerer looked at Yitzhak, puzzled. Why did Miriam's Well seem to have a lasting effect only on this one person? Wait a moment, they still hadn't established the point. "Yitzhak, think back to Monday evening, please. Were you at the Rose Palace that evening? And did you by any chance drink some water from a Pepsi bottle in the fridge there?"

Yitzhak stared at the Rabbi with a blank expression. Why would he ask such a strange thing? "Rose Palace? I haven't been in there in months. I cook for myself while my wife and kids are away."

Feivush asked suddenly, "You didn't happen to drink any water from a well on Motzaei Shabbos, did you?"

"Water from a well?" Yitzhak asked astonished. "There are no wells in Boro Park!"

Rabbi Lerer couldn't believe what he was hearing. The ones that drank from Miriam's Well all seemed to revert to their former selves the next day. Yet this one person, who didn't drink, remains changed? What was going on here? "Why do you still want to move?" he asked.

"I told you, I saw all those guys learning here, I thought I should join them, that's all. They were all talking about how we're all going to die one day, and we have to grab as many mitzvos as we can, including learning Torah and living in the Holy Land. I was so inspired, I thought I should do the same." Yitzhak stole a glance at his watch. "Look, excuse me, I've got to be going. I want to be up for that *shiur,* I mean *chavrusa,* tomorrow morning."

Feivush blurted out, "You can call it a *shiur.* I'll try to make it this time."

All eyes in the room suddenly shifted to Michael, who suddenly turned a shade of red. After shuffling his feet a bit he said, "Okay, you can count on me too."

Yitzhak smiled, and walked out. The second he was out of earshot, Feivush said, "What do you make of it, Rabbi?"

"Yitzhak didn't drink from the well. He didn't get a sudden, unexpected jolt. He simply saw what you were doing, gave it some thought, and decided on his own what he should do. That's why his change lasted and everyone else's didn't."

Rabbi Lerer saw both Michael and Feivush suddenly staring at their shoes. He continued, "*Middos* have to be worked on. Either you're going up or you're going down. That's why Yaakov Avinu dreamed of a ladder. You both got a sudden jolt of inspiration, but since you didn't realize that you'd have to put in effort to keep up the new level, naturally it faded."

Michael and Feivush just looked at each other, realizing they had ruined an outstanding opportunity. Michael quickly stood up, and Feivush asked, "Where are you going?"

"Maybe Yitzhak needs a loan to get him to Eretz Yisrael. Then I'm going straight home. I want to be up for that shiur at 5:30."

Yossi saw a UFO!

One night at dinner Mr. Abels said to his son Yossi, "I ran into your Rebbe last night at a *chasunah.*"

Yossi caught his breath and gulped hard, hoping he wouldn't choke. His father never had a good word for him, and now he was ganging up on him with the Rebbe! How was he going to make it through dinner? Breathe slow, put that bland look back on the face... finally he forced out, "What'd he say?" Maybe it wouldn't be too bad. He'd pulled a B- on the last test, that had to count for something....

Mr. Abels just smiled pleasantly. Yossi wasn't reassured, though: his father was always smiling, but it was never for him. "What's gotten into you?" asked Mr. Abels jokingly. "What's gotten into me?" thought Yossi. "Nothing. Everything's just as usual. Never mind, I'll make it through somehow."

"Your Rebbe only had good things to say," continued Mr. Abels, not noticing the embittered look that had crossed Yossi's face for just one moment. He never did notice things like that. "Rabbi Weinstein thinks that you grasp concepts quickly, and with a little more effort you could be one of the top boys in the class."

Yossi broke into a smile. It was hard to believe, but it seemed that somebody had actually noticed he was trying. After dinner he went to his room to study, beaming.

The next day Yossi suddenly broke a long-standing habit. He said something to his *chavrusa* Moshe: specifically, "I have a *kushya* here." When he had told his *kushya* in full, Moshe's eyes lit up. "Good! That's a real hard one. Let's see if the Rishonim say anything." After they had looked through some *sefarim* without finding an answer, Yossi broke his habit again by proclaiming, "I know what! I'll look it up tonight on the Net."

That evening Yossi turned on his computer and logged onto a *Daf Yomi* website. There was the icon, "Insights on the *Daf*." He clicked on it, quickly found the *daf* he was looking for, and clicked again. Eagerly he scrolled down through the sources displayed, then his face lit up. He lifted his eyebrows and leaned forward to the screen. Yes! His question was answered! After he'd read it again he was sure, and printed out the page. He could hardly wait until tomorrow, when he could share it with Moshe.

Suddenly he heard his mother call, "Yossi! Pick up the phone. Uncle Tzvi's calling!"

Yossi flew to the phone in his room. "How are you, Uncle Tzvi? How are things in Israel?"

"Baruch Hashem, quiet for now. Are we on for this summer?"

"Wow, I'd really love to come. I miss you so much since you moved to Israel. Nobody's taken me fishing since you've left...."

"Nu, so are you coming? There's plenty of fish in Israel."

"Does that mean I get a fishing trip if I come?" Yossi said, and then giggled.

"For you, I always have time," Uncle Tzvi answered. "Didn't we have a good time together in Toronto? Maybe you should book the flight now, you'll get a cheaper fare."

Yossi stammered, "Um, I don't think I can do it. Um, my parents haven't given me a definite answer yet. I — I think maybe they're scared with all the bombings going on." The truth was that they hadn't paid attention to a word he'd said about the summer trip, but he couldn't admit that to Uncle Tzvi.... There was that sinking feeling again in the pit of his stomach. He never could get his parents to listen, or plan with him, or....

Uncle Tzvi said, "Oh, come on! What're they so afraid of? It's just as dangerous in New York."

Yossi rose quickly to his parents' defense. "Well, here we don't have any suicide bombings. At least we haven't since 9/11." He decided to change the subject. "Where are you having the next retreat?"

"I'm negotiating to use a camp in Switzerland, but when they heard it was for Jewish victims of terrorists attacks, they weren't too keen on the idea. I think these guys are anti-Semites, and that means there's nothing I can do with them. I'm going to look for a different location. Look, I'll keep you posted, and I'm going to look forward *davkeh* to seeing you. — Were you doing your homework when I called?"

"Well, yeah, I was."

"Then I don't want to keep you. Please put your mother back on."

The next day Moshe smiled when he saw the printout. As they were going through it, Moshe said offhandedly, "How'd the Knicks do last night?"

Yossi immediately responded, "They won 92-84." He grinned knowingly: "I don't have to tell you — while I was looking up the *daf,* of course I checked out the NBA website."

The next day was one of the first warm days in March. Yossi was glad he could wear a light coat, for the first time in months. Putting it on made him start thinking about summer camp and the start of the baseball season. The world started looking good again.

When he came home from school, Yossi could tell right away that something wasn't right. His father was home from work already. He seemed flustered, upset even, pacing the room while he talked on the cordless phone. Yossi heard him say into the phone, "Get me the next available one. Why not? ... I really don't want to go stand-by. Are you sure that's the only way you can get me on?" Where was Tatteh going?

He saw his mother come in the room, her eyes fixed on the floor. Something was really, really wrong. Then Mama looked up, and Yossi saw that her eyes were puffy and red. He had to know. "What's going on?" he asked, and his voice quavered on the last word.

She looked at him, trying to speak, then said hesitatingly, "We just had a phone call... Uncle Tzvi is dead. He was caught in a suicide bombing in Machaneh Yehudah." She tottered a moment, then continued slowly, almost mechanically. "Tatteh is flying to Israel to help arrange the *levayah.* He'll be sitting *shiv'ah* with Uncle Tzvi's sisters."

Yossi stood there frozen in place. Did he hear right?

How could it be? He'd never see his uncle again? He managed to plop himself on the couch. Words came stumbling out of his mouth. "Uncle Tzvi died? I just spoke to him yesterday! I just spoke to him. He can't be dead."

That night Yossi couldn't sleep. His uncle did so much for the victims of terrorism, and now he was a victim? Where was justice in the world? What about all the children who were depending on him for financial support, and for a chance to pull themselves together at Uncle Tzvi's camp retreats? Why should they have to suffer any more? ... Why should *he* have to suffer this way? The only one that ever loved him was dead. Would anyone ever talk to him again? Would anyone ever laugh with him, listen to him? Suddenly Yossi was sobbing into his pillow and couldn't stop. He wept on and on late into the night, and nobody came to comfort him.

Next day in yeshivah, Yossi was too shaken up to concentrate. He kept the bland look on his face, though; he had to survive somehow, and if he broke down no one would care, no one would listen.... Even during his *chavrusa* with Moshe he was distant, far off in his pain. Always he'd found an answer to his *kushyos* in the *sefarim*, but this question didn't seem to have an answer. He knew how it was formulated: *tzaddik v'ra lo*, when bad things happen to good people. He knew it was all discussed in the *sefarim*, but words on a page didn't do anything to stop his heart from aching. Why should his uncle, who did so much for victims of terrorism, become the next victim? His uncle, whom he loved so much? Yossi's head started spinning; he felt as if his world had just shattered.

That night he tried to review but found that he still couldn't focus. "Maybe," he thought, "I could come up with something again on the *Daf Yomi* website." He managed to get to the site and find the right *daf,* but still he couldn't concentrate; what he read on the screen wasn't making any sense. His mind was still wandering, lost in its private desert. "Doesn't God punish and reward *middah k'neged middah,* measure for measure? How could this be a just punishment? What did my uncle do to deserve it?" There was no one he could ask, he knew that. Nobody would even pay attention to his question, nobody would even hear him asking it....

He stared blankly at the screen for a few minutes, then finally realized he wasn't getting anywhere. He felt a sudden urge to escape — anything to keep from thinking about Uncle Tzvi. Almost instinctively, his fingers clicked the mouse a few times, and the NBA site came up. The moment he saw the familiar basketball player on the screen he began to relax. He leaned back in his chair, sighing quietly, one hand poised on the mouse. He read a few articles, checked the scores of games in progress, and even looked at the standings of the Italian and Israeli leagues. After he while he glanced at the time posted at the bottom left corner of the screen.

"11:28 PM? Huh? Is it that late already?" A glance at the clock on his wall confirmed it. He suddenly noticed that his eyes were tired from reading for so long. Quickly he shut down for the night.

The next night Yossi logged on again to the site, but after a few minutes he yawned. There was nothing new since last night.

"No problem," he thought, and switched to a Web-search engine, where he looked for yet another basketball-related site. What he found at "yourteam.com" amazed him. This site was a fantasy league that allowed him to own a team, pick the players, and advance in the standings based on how his players actually performed in each month's NBA games. He spent the next half-hour registering and selecting the players for his team. Wow, he could actually feel like an owner!

He stayed up that night past eleven o'clock to get all the scores from the day's games. The next morning he woke up early to check the scores of the West Coast games. As his father's *shiv'ah* trip dragged on through the next two weeks, the NBA suddenly became Yossi's passion. He still learned half-heartedly with Moshe, the highlight of his day became lunch, when he could talk about players and teams with the yeshivah's sports expert, Baruch Hertz. Only then his face took on an animated look.

Walking to Shacharis the next morning, Yossi tapped Baruch on the shoulder and whispered, "I woke up late. How many points did Jordan score?"

"I think around twelve, something like that."

Yossi smiled sardonically. "Twelve points? That's it? He ought to retire for good already."

After the third week his father returned, haggard and pale, and the house regained a modicum of normality. The question of "how that could happen to Uncle Tzvi" still bothered Yossi, but since he didn't know an answer to the problem he could only ignore it. He just needed something to get his mind off of it. That meant more basketball.

Now every night after dinner Yossi went straight to his room. "I've got a lot of homework," he told his parents. They never minded when he said that, never even asked what the homework was. They certainly never offered any help. For that matter, they never looked in his room to ask how he was doing. Did they even hear him saying he had homework?... Yossi stopped the thoughts abruptly when the familiar sinking feeling started in his stomach. He just wasn't going to think this way, it never did any good. He put the impassive look back on his face, the one he kept there almost all the time.

He sometimes felt guilty, though, for spending so much time in the closed room, with the computer on, away from his learning. He hadn't planned for things to come out like this, but he was hooked and didn't know how to stop. Because if he did stop, then that problem nagging at the back of his mind would come to the front, and — he couldn't afford that.

His Rebbe, Rabbi Weinstein, noticed Yossi was not the same *bachur* he was a few months earlier. He didn't seem interested in learning any more.

"Just sit down for an hour tonight and look over the Gemara in the English translation," Rabbi Weinstein begged him one day after class. It never occurred to him to ask Yossi what was bothering him. He hadn't heard about his uncle being killed. Yossi mumbled, "Okay, I'll try," but once he got to his room and saw the computer, he went straight over and logged on to some basketball sites.

Things only got worse from then on. Soon Yossi wasn't even keeping up with the rest of the class. Naturally, it showed in his grades.

Yossi was in the kitchen eating Crunchy Nut Cornflakes for supper one evening when he heard the phone. His mother picked it up on the first ring. He only heard half the conversation, but that was enough to know he was in trouble.

"Who is this? Rabbi Weinstein?" Yossi cringed. He froze. "Is everything all right with Yossi?" For a moment he wondered what his Rebbe could want, but quickly he figured it out. Now his stomach was sinking again. He didn't like that feeling, he never could get used to it.

After his mother hung up she looked at Yossi, who had put his impassive look back on and was now very busy reading the back of the cereal box. "That was your Rebbe," she said in a flat voice.

Yossi's eyes were glued to the back of the box.

"He said you're not paying attention in class. You've done poorly on your last few tests, and he's concerned. What's going on, Yossi?"

He looked up for a fleeting moment. "The tests have been really hard," was all he could muster, his eyes already back on the cereal box.

"Are you studying, Yossi? What are you doing all evening in your room?" No answer. His mother shrugged and turned back to the sink, and there was silence again.

At ten o'clock that night, Mendy knocked on his younger brother Yossi's door. As usual, Yossi hit the hot key to hide the site he was looking at, then said, "Come in."

Mendy said simply, "Mom and Dad want you in the kitchen."

"Uh oh!" Yossi thought, as he felt his heartbeat increase. "No way around this one," he thought. The bland look came over his face as he walked downstairs.

He found his parents sitting at the kitchen table drinking tea. They told him to sit down. After talking plainly about his grades, his father said, "We have no choice but to take the modem off your computer. You can only use it for writing and studying."

Yossi was shocked. "No Web?" How could they do that to him? "For how long?" This time he couldn't help but look upset. He was.

Mr. Abels didn't notice that, but all the same he thought a moment how to be fair. "You can have it back on Rosh Chodesh Nissan," he answered.

Yossi said nothing, just got up and walked away, crushed. He spent the next night staring at the computer screen, watching the flying toasters. He felt as if he had lost his best friend.

Over the next few days Yossi tried to keep up with his studies, but he found that he was only interested, more than ever before, in schmoozing with his friends in the lunchroom. After all, it was very difficult to follow the

NBA without his Web link. He started to spend more and more time schmoozing, at every available moment. Soon he found himself over at his friends' houses in the evenings, using their computer links and talked non-stop about basketball. His parents didn't seem to notice. As Yossi was at home less and less of the day, he sometimes felt a bit like a refugee. But he didn't care, as long as he didn't have to think about The Problem. It never occurred to him that in a way he was a refugee, fleeing from troubles beyond his capacity to deal with.

Baruch sat next to Yossi on the bus one morning. It was a warm spring day, and Yossi heard the birds chirping for the first time since Sukkos. Then Baruch leaned over to him and whispered, "Wanna go to the Yankee game today?"

Yossi sat back in his chair. He didn't really feel like going to Rabbi Weinstein's class. He was still angry with him for tattling to his parents. The words came tumbling out of his mouth: "Who's playing?"

"The A's."

"So... why not?" thought Yossi. "I've never cut school before, but there's a first time for everything."

"Okay," he whispered, as an evil smile replaced the usual stolid look on his face.

"The game starts at 1:30," Baruch said excitedly. "We'll grab the Monsey bus, get off near Penn station, and take a couple of subways to the Bronx. If we leave by ten, we should be there for the first pitch."

Baruch and Yossi were tired when they finally made it

to the Yankee Stadium box office, where a shock awaited them. For some reason they had thought tickets in the bleachers would be around $1.50. They weren't: the price was $10.00 a seat! "Too many millionaire players," Yossi thought.

By the third inning the Yanks had fallen behind 8-1. Yossi started spending some time reading the articles in his scorecard. He decided that he liked the fast pace of basketball better. In comparison, this game was dull. And it didn't help having your team behind by seven runs.

Suddenly Yossi felt something hit him on his head. It didn't feel like a baseball; it was more like the spitballs he used to throw in first grade. He reached up to touch his yarmulke just as he felt another one hit his hand. Bringing his hand down, he found a peanut shell sticking to it. "How did that get here?" he wondered. Was someone — could someone be throwing peanut shells at him? He quickly turned around and saw two men in their mid-thirties, sitting about four rows behind them. One wearing a "Polin Chainsaws" baseball hat, the other's hat said "CAT—caterpillar tractors." Both had large unkempt beards and lumberjack shirts. Were they the ones throwing peanut shells at him? Yossi stared at them for a few moments, but they just sat back watching the game while munching their peanuts, smugly pretending to be unaware of any wrongdoing.

The second Yossi turned around he felt himself again being pelted. He felt the anger building inside him. He felt like yelling at those two rednecks, but did he want to make a scene? Was it worth a fight with some rednecks who might be stronger than he was?

Baruch had seen what happened. He just said calmly, "Let's change seats." When they stood up and began to walk to the aisle, Yossi caught a glance of the rednecks congratulating each other.

They took seats down the right-field line, where it was much more secluded. After one more inning the game was getting more and more boring; Yossi realized at last that he just didn't feel like being there any longer. He said, "I've had enough. Let's get outta here."

On the subway back to Penn station, Baruch said, "Next time we should wear baseball caps also."

Yossi said, "I don't want to go anywhere where I have to wear a disguise. I guess that's not a place for us to go. — At least we won't be back home too late." Sure enough, the two arrived back in Monsey by the end of the afternoon.

As Rosh Chodesh Nissan approached, Yossi tried his best to keep in line. He even managed an 80 on his next test. With the NBA finals approaching he really needed his modem back, so much that he even opened an ArtScroll Gemara a few times in the evening.

The next day in class Rabbi Weinstein asked, "Rosh Chodesh Nissan is a special day. One may not fast on Rosh Chodesh, but on Rosh Chodesh Nissan it is permitted — and this is the only day in all of Nissan that we are permitted to fast. Does anyone know why?"

Yossi raised his hand. Rabbi Weinstein called on him with a smile, and Yossi said, "Death of Nadav and Avihu."

"Excellent," Rabbi Weinstein replied. "That's correct."

After class, Yossi told Baruch, "I read about that last night. It may be a sad day, but not for me. I'm getting my modem back tonight!"

With his modem reattached, Yossi felt like a *chasan* on the day of his wedding. He immediately plugged into the latest standings in the NBA, and was upset to see that Jordan was still having a lousy year. "Definitely can't wait 'til he retires again," he commented under his breath.

Now that Yossi had his drug back, Gemara once again took a back seat. To be specific, it sat there unopened for the next several nights.

Over the next few days Rabbi Weinstein had plenty of opportunities to notice how once again Yossi was off in cloudland. But why? The best guess he could make was that Yossi was totally interested in something other than class. In fact he was quite correct. Yossi had his whole mind on something quite different than Gemara.

A few days before Pesach break, Baruch once again sat next to Yossi on the bus with that mischievous look on his face. "I've got another idea for today...."

Yossi interrupted him. "I'm not going back to Yankee Stadium to get pelted by those *goyim*."

Baruch had a ready reply, "We'll get better seats. I found out that no respectable person sits in the bleachers."

"Forget it.... Hey, I've got an idea."

"What?"

"It's really nice outside. Let's get a bus from Suffern and go for a hike on Bear Mountain."

"A hike?" Baruch sounded intrigued.

"Why not? We have our lunches already, and we'll pick up a few bottles of water."

Well, why not?

The trip to Bear Mountain was quicker than they thought it would be, and they got there by ten o'clock. The bus dropped them off at the main parking lot near the ball fields and swimming pool. Yossi and Baruch bought a few sodas and potato chips at the refreshment stand, and then went to the Main Office to get directions to one of the hiking trails.

The park ranger showed them the trails marked on a map under the glass counter, recommending a short hike up one of the hills. But, he told them, they would have to walk about a half a mile to get to the starting point. This particular trail was worth it, he said, because it led to a scenic overview. The ranger told them, "On a clear day like today, you can even make out the lines of Manhattan."

The boys thanked the Ranger and started walking down Seven Lakes Drive. A few minutes along the way a jeep stopped next to them, and the driver rolled down his window. "Where are you fellows headed?"

"The hiking trail down this road," Yossi replied.

"C'mon in, I'll give you a lift."

About four minutes later the jeep dropped them off. "Thanks a lot, Mister," Yossi said politely as he got out. It didn't take long to find the trail marker, and after a few minutes on the trail Yossi felt exhilarated. He loved the feeling of being surrounded by green. He took in a deep breath and let the air fill his lungs. He was grateful he hadn't gone to the ball game today.

The pair walked slowly up the path, which thankfully was not very steep. After about fifteen minutes of hiking they rested, overlooking a beautiful green valley below. Looking up, Yossi squinted. He saw a cloudy figure of something, off in the distance. He stared at it for a few moments, then broke into a smile. "Look at that!" he yelled, and pointed. "Just like the ranger said, there's Manhattan."

They both stared for a few moments. Yossi was in awe. He had never seen the far-off outline of Manhattan like that before. "The trip was worth it," he thought, "just for this sight." They hiked on for a while, then stopped to take a drink from the bottle of Pepsi, enjoying the view. Almost instinctively, both stood up at the same time and walked farther along the path.

After another ten minutes they came to a small cliff fringed with trees. The view from it wasn't as picturesque as the first one, but beautiful nonetheless. Yossi squinted, and felt a little upset when he couldn't make out Manhattan any longer. But there, in the distance, he saw a bridge spanning a wide river. "What's that?" he asked Baruch, pointing.

"It must be the Tappan Zee Bridge," answered Baruch. "Just to the left, there, that must be Nyack, and —"

"Look!" Yossi interrupted him with shock in his voice. He stood there with his eyes bulging, his tongue hanging out of his mouth, one hand on his yarmulke, the other pointing at an object in the sky. Baruch looked up. There was something silvery, oval-shaped, with a hump on its top, hovering in the sky! Thoughts went flying through Baruch's head: "What is that thing? What's it doing up there? When did it get there?"

Yossi stared and felt his heart starting to do somersaults. "What is that thing? It looks like... like... a flying saucer!" Baruch stood alongside of Yossi, their eyes glued to the UFO. Suddenly Yossi found his vocal cords. "Camera. Camera. Did you bring a camera?"

Baruch was in a trance and didn't seem to have heard a word. Yossi nudged him with his elbow and yelled, "Take a picture!"

"What?"

"Take a picture!"

"I don't have a camera."

The boys silently went back to staring at the flying saucer. The silence lasted for about thirty seconds; then suddenly the saucer sped to their left, making no sound, moving faster than any object they ever saw move in the sky, until some trees blocked their view.

"C'mon, lets follow it!" Yossi commanded. They began to run along the cliff, but thickets of trees slowed them down. They tried to navigate through the forest while still looking at the sky, but now the trees tripped them up. The forest was thick here. When they came to a patch of bramble-bushes they realized they couldn't go on. They scanned the sky between the branches for a few moments, but there was no sign of the flying saucer anywhere. Disappointed, they slowly turned back and went to the spot where they first saw the UFO. Once again they looked out at the Tappan Zee Bridge. All they saw this time was a peaceful spring day.

The boys stood there for a moment in silence. Then Yossi looked at Baruch, who still had the same shocked expression on his face. "What was that thing?" he asked.

Baruch shook his head. "I don't know," he said. He was bewildered, his heart was still racing, and his mind wasn't thinking coherently. Slowly Yossi said, "It had to be an alien flying saucer. Other people around Bear Mountain must have also seen it. People must be panicking. I'll bet TV crews are there at the Main Office right now." Suddenly the trance snapped and he felt excited. "C'mon, let's go see what's happening!"

In a flash Yossi turned to run down the trail, with Baruch closely behind him. When they arrived at the road, about fifteen minutes later, it was deserted.

They stopped for a moment to catch their breath. "Where's that Jeep now that we need him?" Yossi panted. A few moments later he straightened up and said, "C'mon, let's get going. Who knows what's happening down there?" Although he was exhausted from running down the mountain, Baruch pushed himself to follow Yossi. But his legs wouldn't obey, and he trailed behind.

He barely managed to call out, "Wait up! I can't go so fast." With no alternative, the two settled into a quick walk. They tried to hitch a ride, but the few cars on the isolated mountain road just passed them by.

When they finally got back to the main park area they were shocked by what they saw. People were playing Frisbee and roller-skating, as if nothing had happened! There was no panic, no TV cameras, and no reporters.

They stared blankly for a few moments, until Yossi said, "C'mon, follow me!" and ran towards the main office.

They barged in and found the ranger sitting at his small wooden desk, reading a book about bird-watching. When he heard someone come in panting, he looked up, expecting an emergency. He recognized the boys immediately, and was about to say, "Back so soon?" but Yossi beat him to it. "Did anyone else see it?" he asked excitedly.

The ranger looked at him blankly. "See what?"

"The UFO! Didn't anyone here see it?"

The ranger squinted and pulled back from his desk, then asked with a smile, "You guys are kidding me, right?"

Baruch interjected, "Didn't anyone else report it? I'm sure lots of people saw it."

The ranger leaned forward with a puzzled expression on his face. "Are you boys serious? Nobody reported anything."

Yossi explained, "We were out hiking and saw a flying saucer. It was silvery and oval, and it sped through the sky, and we...."

The ranger lifted his hand in dismissal. "Oh, I'm sure it was nothing. You know we're right near West Point, where the military academy is. Maybe it was some sort of experimental aircraft or a helicopter or something."

Yossi shook his head. "I never saw anything move that fast in the sky. Besides, why would there be special aircraft at West Point? It's an Army officer's academy, not Air Force. They don't even have an airfield there."

"Well, maybe it was just a shooting star or something like that," the ranger said reasonably.

Seeing that they weren't getting anywhere, Yossi said, "C'mon, let's ask some other people."

Baruch saw an old man sitting on a park bench listening to a small radio. He said, "Excuse me, Sir, but did you hear anything about a flying saucer?"

The man looked at them as if they were crazy. "Have you boys been drinking?" he asked accusingly. Yossi yanked Baruch by the arm and they continued walking. By now Yossi was beginning to feel a little ridiculous. They walked along the grass field hoping to spot someone staring upwards, or at least listening to the radio.

Baruch motioned up ahead when they saw a couple having a picnic on the edge of the grass with a radio on. Baruch thought about asking them about the flying saucer, until he heard the rock music coming from the radio. "Maybe there'll be an interruption for a news bulletin," he said softly. Yossi shook his head not to bother. They continued wandering in a daze until Yossi suddenly realized they were near the refreshment stand. He had an idea. "Hey, the guy had a TV in there. Maybe he heard something."

The boys walked in and immediately looked up at the TV in the corner. It had on "Wheel of Fortune." Undeterred, they stood in front of the vendor nervously. He turned and asked mechanically, "What'll it be, boys?"

Yossi said, "Um, nothing. We wanted to ask you about a flying saucer...."

The vendor opened up his freezer and handed over a round ice-cream sandwich. "Flying Saucer, $2.50."

Baruch cut in, "What we want to know is if you heard

about one today. We saw it, and it flew across the sky like a rocket...."

The vendor reached again in the freezer, and slap! Two ices appeared on the counter. "Red Rocket, $1.50."

The boys turned their backs, leaving the ices on the counter, and walked out.

By silent agreement they headed for the bus stop. Nobody else saw it? They were in a daze. How could it be? Did no one believe them?

The boys didn't speak much on the return trip. When he finally made it home, around five o'clock, Yossi went to his room right away and checked the *Times* and CNN websites. He couldn't believe it! Nothing was even mentioned! There wasn't anything on *The Rockland Journal-News* website either. What was going on here? He picked up the phone and called Baruch. "There's nothing on any news websites!"

Baruch answered, "Well, that means that I have to report it."

Yossi hesitated. He didn't want his name in the paper. "Um, do me one favor. Leave my name out of it. I've had enough with the people at the park thinking I'm crazy."

Baruch agreed reluctantly, then hung up the phone and called Information. After he got the number for the Rockland *Journal-News* he dialed it, only to hear a recording telling him business hours were from eight to five. "Shouldn't newspapers be open twenty-four hours?" he wondered as he put down the receiver.

Yossi couldn't even think of going to bed that night, he was so rattled with the questions. Who was flying those flying saucers? Where did they come from? Where were they going? What did they look like? Were they the famous "Little Green Men"? They must be more intelligent than us, or else how could they build such a spacecraft? If they could build such a spacecraft, were they planning an invasion of some sort?

Around ten-thirty he called up Baruch again. Baruch said he'd had more or less the same response from everyone in his family: either he was exaggerating, or he saw a natural phenomenon like a shooting star or a comet.

The next morning, a few minutes after eight, Baruch called up the Rockland *Journal-News*. The operator connected him with a member of the staff, and Baruch said right away, "Hello, Journal-News? Have I got a scoop for you!"

"A scoop? Yeah, sure, what is it?"

"I'm telling you, it's a headline grabber."

"Yeah, yeah, okay, kid. What is it?"

Why did the man sound bored? That was funny. "My friend and I saw a UFO!"

Baruch was upset when he heard a sigh. "Another one? Listen, kid, you got any pictures of it?"

"Pictures? Well, no. We were just hiking on Bear Mountain. Neither of us had a camera."

"Well, let me know if you come up with pictures. And next time you go UFO hunting, have enough common sense to take along a camera!"

"Wait! We weren't UFO hunting —" Baruch only heard the dial tone.

The next day in school Yossi came out of davening and gaped. There was a small crowd around Baruch, who seemed to be enjoying the limelight. "It hovered in front of us for thirty seconds! It sped through the sky, faster than any rocket!" Yossi realized he should have asked Baruch last night not to spread the story too much, but now it was too late.

As Yossi walked into Rabbi Weinstein's class that morning, someone called out, "Did you hear? Yossi saw a UFO!" Another said, "Did you put your phasers on stun for any Klingons today?" Everyone laughed, while Yossi stared at his desk, red in the face.

At lunch that day, Yossi did not appreciate the sudden popularity he'd developed. He could tell from the stares and snickers that people were talking about him. Exaggerated claims of him and Baruch seeing aliens and making contact were going around the yeshivah. When he finally made it to the lunch room, Yossi was hoping Baruch would talk about basketball. He sighed when he saw him giving another report of what they'd seen.

Then Yossi stopped short: one of the boys listening was Sender Rosen — a short, shy boy with thick plastic glasses who always kept to himself. Today he suddenly wanted to hear the whole story. This was getting weirder all the time.

Yossi sat alone at the side; he only wanted to be left alone. Suddenly he felt a tap on his shoulder, and was amazed to find Sender standing to his right. "I just heard about what you guys saw. I saw a report about UFOs on 'The X-Files.' Maybe you should contact them."

Yossi told him that he really didn't need any extra publicity, but Sender went right on, "I have a lot of science-fiction books at home, maybe I'll bring you one tomorrow?" Yossi smiled crookedly and thought, "Just what I need — to be seen carrying science-fiction books around the yeshivah. They'll probably put me away!" He got rid of Sender with some muttered excuse, and was glad to finish his lunch in peace. He had *bentsched* and was about to go outside when he heard from another table, "Hey Yossi? Seen any flying cups today to go along with your flying saucer?"

Yossi was glad when the day was over. He took a seat at the back of the school bus and hoped nobody would bother him. Nobody did, and he was left reflecting that this was the best thing that had happened the whole day.

When he got home, after saying hello to his mother and barely catching her "Mendy is coming this Shabbos," he ran straight to his room. Once the door was closed he lay down on his bed and stared at the ceiling. Finally, complete peace and quiet.

As he lay there, suddenly he thought of something. "Is there intelligent life outside of earth? But how could that be? How could there be intelligent beings on distant planets? The Torah was given to the Jewish people, as an instruction book telling us how to live in *this* world. Do aliens have a different Torah for their world? Did they have their own revelation at their own Har Sinai on their planet? Would that make them their planet's chosen people?" That thought made him giggle. "We have distant relatives, they live on planet Tralfamadore," he thought fuzzily as he fell asleep.

The next day Yossi stayed after class for a few minutes, while Rabbi Weinstein was putting his Gemara in his attaché case.

"Rabbi?"

He looked up, surprised. "Yes, Yossi?"

"What would Chazal say about life on other planets?"

Rabbi Weinstein stood there, motionless a moment while thinking. "There wouldn't be any reason for anything to be out there. This is the only world."

"But how could they build flying saucers if they're not even there?" asked Yossi, in total confusion.

"Who says there are such things as flying saucers?"

"Didn't you hear about it? I thought everyone knew. Baruch and I saw one the other day!"

"Oh, I'm sure it was nothing. Maybe it was some new type of advertising blimp. I'm sorry, but I'm running late. We can continue this tomorrow," he said, as he grabbed his coat and walked quickly to the classroom door.

"Well," thought Yossi, "Rabbi Weinstein knows about Gemara, but he doesn't know much about this." Where could he find the answer to this *kushya?* How could there be UFOs?

The next day in school, Sender again came over to Yossi at the lunch table. Was he going to ask for his autograph? But Sender simply pulled a book out of his knapsack and said, "I brought this for you." A Star Wars novel? Yossi was shocked when Sender handed him a sefer: *The Aryeh Kaplan Reader.* "What's this?"

"I thought you might want to read it. It has an article about extraterrestrial life. You can bring it back tomorrow," Sender said.

Yossi smiled. "Just what I wanted. Thanks so much," he said to Sender, who was all smiles now.

Thankfully, today there was far less heckling — many students were getting fed up with corny flying-saucer jokes.

Around nine o'clock that night, Yossi was at his computer desk reading the Aryeh Kaplan article for the fourth time when he heard a knock on his bedroom door.

"Come in," he said, his eyes still on the pages.

"What's this about UFOs?" his brother asked. Once again Yossi told the whole story about his hike, what he saw, how everyone at Bear Mountain and the yeshivah acted since.

When he'd finished, Mendy was silent for a few moments, then simply said, "That's some story. You sure that's what you saw?"

Yossi emphatically said, "Positive."

"Sure sounds weird. I don't blame others for not believing you. They shouldn't make fun of you, though."

Eventually Mendy noticed the book lying open. "What're you reading there? A UFO book?"

"No, actually it's the *Aryeh Kaplan Reader*. It has an article about extraterrestrial life."

"What's he say?"

"He's not very clear. He quotes some sources for and against the existence of life on other planets, and the Zohar says it does exist — or that's what he says, anyway.

He also says each *tzaddik* will someday be given his own planet, with its entire population, just 'to enhance his spiritual growth.' I don't get that part; I mean, it doesn't make much sense. A *talmid chacham* is going to rule over a planet of alien beings, and that's going to enhance his spiritual growth? Well, anyway, I was hoping he'd deal with UFOs, but he doesn't mention them."

Mendy thought a moment, then said, "I just remembered something. There was a guy named Simchah Whitelaw he was a head counselor with me at Camp Greenwood last summer. I think now he's a teen counselor. He knew a lot about UFOs — on sleep-outs sometimes he used to talk about them. Maybe you should give him a call."

Yossi looked excited. "How did he know so much? Where is he? How can I get hold of him?"

"Calm down. He lives in Queens. I'll look for his number."

Mendy went to his room, and a minute later came back with a number on a piece of paper. Yossi quickly grabbed the paper out of Mendy's hand, ran to the phone and dialed. Unfortunately, he got the answering machine. "What should I say?" he thought, as suddenly he realized he only had a few seconds to decide. When he heard the beep he blurted out, "This message is for Simchah Whitelaw. My name is Yossi Abels and I live in Monsey and you know my brother Mendy from camp and he said you know about UFOs and stuff like that and my friend and me saw this flying saucer the other day so I wanted to ask you..."

Suddenly the beep sounded, and the line went dead. Yossi stared at the phone for a few moments before he hung it up. How foolish he must have sounded! He considered calling back, but decided that would only make things worse. He walked away from the phone feeling disgusted with himself, and went back to his room. Instinctively he turned on his computer.

He wasn't in the mood to look at basketball scores right now; but what did he want to look at? With the help of a search engine he found a website devoted to UFOs. Yossi broke into a smile when he saw the contents. It listed daily UFO sightings, by state and by country. "More people see UFOs than I imagined," he thought. He clicked on New York, and was surprised that although several sightings were reported, there were none for the date when he saw one. Just then he spotted a three-page form to be submitted by anyone who had seen a UFO. Yossi answered all the questions on the form and posted it. His interest sparked, he read some of the articles, including several by Steve Whitelaw. "Wow! I'll bet that's the same guy as Simchah," he said to himself.

Friday afternoon, Yossi came home from shopping at Wesley Kosher with shopping bags in his arms. Before he had a chance to put them down, Mendy ran up to him and said, "Simchah Whitelaw called you back about half an hour ago! He said he's coming to Monsey this Shabbos, and he'll come over on Motzaei Shabbos around nine. He wants to talk to you and anyone else who saw that UFO."

Yossi's face broke into a smile. Finally, somebody who'd believe him! Maybe he could answer some questions, too.

Yossi was fidgety all that Shabbos. He considered

walking to the Brewer area of Monsey, where Simchah was staying, but the thought of a forty-five-minute walk in the rain made him change his mind. As soon as Shabbos ended his mood crashed. He was expecting disappointment and frustration — it seemed that was all he'd had since he saw the UFO. Every time the phone rang he was sure it would bring the message that Simchah wasn't coming. In desperation he went up to his room and turned on the computer.

At a quarter to nine Yossi heard the doorbell ring. His mother called, "Yossi, someone's here for you!" He bolted downstairs, and was a little disappointed to see Baruch standing in the doorway with his raincoat dripping. After a moment, though, he remembered his manners and said, "C'mon in, let me take your coat. Ya want a hot drink?"

Yossi and Baruch were drinking hot chocolate in the kitchen fifteen minutes later when they heard the doorbell ring. Mendy answered it.

"Shalom Aleichem, Sim; c'mon in."

"A gut voch."

Yossi left his hot chocolate on the kitchen table and ran into the entranceway. Simchah was taller than his brother, had short black hair and an unkempt beard. He was carrying a manila folder in his hand.

Mendy said, "This is my friend from camp, Simchah Whitelaw. Sim, this is the guy you came to see, my brother Yossi."

After the two shook hands, Simchah asked right away, "Anyone else with you?"

"My friend Baruch Cooperman. He's in the kitchen drinking hot chocolate. Want some?"

Simchah smiled. "Maybe later. I really came to hear what you guys saw. Where's a place we could talk?"

Yossi said simply, "My room, I guess." Yossi called Baruch, who took the last swigs from his mug and mumbled his *berachah acharonah*. The three marched upstairs.

Yossi and Baruch sat on the bed, while Simchah took the chair from the computer desk and swiveled it in front of the two boys. "I have a standard interview," he began, "that I do with people who've seen UFOs."

Yossi asked, "You do this sort of thing often?"

Simchah waved his hand. "I used to do some writing for a website."

Yossi's ears pricked up. "So Steve Whitelaw was you? I guessed that."

Simchah said simply, "I went by that name before I did *teshuvah*."

Yossi explained, "I read some of your articles last night." Now he wanted to ask how someone who worked for a UFO website became religious. But it was more important for Simchah to do the interview.

He got right on with it. "Did anyone that you know of, besides you two, see the UFO?"

Baruch said, "No."

"When did you see it?"

Yossi said, "This past Tuesday, at around two o'clock in the afternoon."

"Tuesday?" Simchah asked with surprise in his voice. "Weren't you supposed to be in yeshivah?"

Yossi blushed a little. "Well, I guess you could say we were playing hooky."

"I see." Simchah smiled, and added in an undertone, "I've missed a few days myself. — So, exactly what did you see?"

By this time Baruch had it down to a set speech. One more time, in vivid detail, he told Simchah what they saw. Yossi added a few points about how the object zoomed through the sky. Once Baruch finished, Yossi added, "I submitted a report on-line last night. You want to see a copy?"

Simchah excitedly said, "Yeah!" so Yossi went to his desk, opened a drawer, and handed Simchah three sheets of paper. Simchah took one look and commented, "Ah yes, from the website I used to write for."

Yossi actually sat on his hands, he was so eaten up with the desire to ask Simchah how he became religious. Did it have anything to do with UFOs? He'd met many *baalei teshuvah,* but never one that had come to Torah from a flying saucer. It would be really weird if that were the case here. He controlled himself, though; he knew that first he had to allow Simchah to read the report and do his interview.

As Simchah read the pages, Yossi and Baruch became increasingly fidgety. Simchah finally looked up to ask Yossi exactly what position the flying saucer had held in the sky, and what they had seen in the background. Once he'd finished, he swiveled the chair back to the computer desk, put down Yossi's report, and picked up the manila envelope he was carrying. He opened it, stood up, and unfolded a map of Rockland County on the bed, between where Yossi and Baruch were sitting.

Simchah cleared his throat. "Now, you say that you saw the Tappan Zee Bridge in the background, right?"

Yossi nodded.

Simchah put his finger on the map just below the words "Bear Mountain" and said, "That would have been southeast from where you two were standing. Let's assume you were standing right over here and looking southeast. About where would the flying saucer have been?"

Yossi and Baruch looked at the map for a few moments, and didn't know quite what to answer. Eventually Yossi put an uncertain finger on the map and said, "I guess it would have been somewhere around here."

Simchah stood up and looked where Yossi's finger was. He announced, "According to that, the UFO was hovering somewhere between Congers and New City." He looked up at Yossi and Baruch with raised eyebrows and softly said, "How come nobody in either of those places saw it?"

There was an uncomfortable silence for a few moments, enough to make Yossi feel uneasy. Then Simchah continued, "From the approximate coordinates you've given me, it would have been visible in Nanuet, Nyack, and probably even Monsey. If we go one step further, these towns are all within fifteen miles of the Hudson River. At the height you put in your report and the ideal weather conditions you had last Tuesday, the flying saucer would have been visible to towns on the other side of the Hudson as well, like Irvington and Tarrytown. Close to half a million people were in eyeshot of your flying saucer; yet nobody reported seeing it but you two."

Yossi and Baruch didn't know what to say. They felt as

if they were on trial, with the prosecuting attorney stacking evidence against them, while they had nothing but their say-so. Suddenly Baruch said, "Maybe nobody else was looking."

Simchah sat back in his chair. "Did you ever hear of the *Hindenburg?* It was a huge blimp, the largest airship ever built. It exploded in New Jersey in 1937. Anyway, when it first flew over New York, thousands of people reported seeing it, even from many miles away. The entire crowd at a Giants-Dodgers game saw it that day, in fact they were so carried away they stopped the game. Yet nobody else saw this UFO but you two. Why do you think that could be?"

Yossi clutched his fists and felt his pulse increasing. Whose side was this guy on? Did he come here to make fools out of them? To make them out to be liars?

Yossi blurted out, "I'm telling you, we both saw it! Do you think we made this whole thing up?"

"No, of course not. What you're saying is no more than what a lot of other people have said, and I have no reason to think that so many people are all liars. In fact, they couldn't be, because liars always say different things, and UFO-sighters all report the same things.

"According to all my findings, only a few people ever see a flying saucer. Entire towns, or even a whole block, never see them all together. I mean, if that thing is up there hanging in the sky, within the line of view for thousands or even millions of people, wouldn't there be massive reports? When it streaks through the sky, how come nobody in the next town sees it? We hardly even get reports of it being seen from different angles, like some seeing it from the front and at the same time others seeing from behind. It's just a couple of people standing in the same place.

"The position in the sky you saw the UFO is also typical. People almost never report seeing a UFO directly overhead. They're usually seen just at the angle you two reported. And people never, never see a UFO close up. It's always seen at a distance, again, the way you say you saw it."

Baruch leaned back on his hands, dazed, but Yossi felt great. Someone finally believed him! All this stuff was very puzzling, however. He'd never thought of it. *Why* hadn't more people seen the UFO? If it was in the sky, hovering for so long, wouldn't everybody...?

His thoughts were interrupted by Simchah. "Now, after the flying saucer zoomed through the sky, did it make a sonic boom?"

Yossi looked at Baruch for a moment, and then looked at Simchah with a puzzled look on his face. "What's a sonic boom?"

"It's the noise made by an airplane when it passes the speed of sound. It happens because the air gets pushed so hard in front of the plane, and it sounds like a bomb exploding in the air. I still remember the first time I heard one, when I was learning in Jerusalem. I was walking on Jaffa Road and this loud explosion came from the sky. I was certain it was a terrorist bombing! I was shocked when everyone in the street just kept on walking as if nothing had happened. When I asked, in my broken Hebrew, I was told it was just a 'sonic boom,' and then I had to go and find out what that was.

"Eventually you learn to tell one when you hear it, but in this case I just want to know: did you hear any loud boom?"

Baruch's forehead wrinkled, while Yossi lifted one eyebrow as he thought. Then he said, "No, we didn't hear anything like that."

"Yet it's a fact of nature. The shock wave caused by any object reaching supersonic speed makes that noise. The way you describe the UFO, it must have broken the sound barrier. Yet it didn't make any boom. UFOs never do. None of the people I've interviewed ever reported a sonic boom."

By now, Yossi was totally baffled. Why didn't anyone else see it? Why don't UFOs make a sonic boom? After a few seconds of silence a thought occurred to him. "How do you know all this?"

"Simple. When I worked for that website, I interviewed a lot of people who claimed to have seen UFOs. Everyone was convinced that alien beings from another planet were piloting the flying saucers, but that didn't make sense to me. I mean, there were so many problems with that: a UFO is seen only by a few and not by others, it never makes a sonic boom, and is never seen directly overhead or close up. Why would that be?

"And what planets were they from? Since UFOs appear in so many different sizes and shapes, were they all from different planets? These questions bothered me, but I had no answers for them.

"Around the same time, I saw a report that Israel had the highest per capita rate of UFO sightings of any country. That got me thinking: was there anything special about my being Jewish?" Yossi stirred in expectation: was he about to hear how Simchah had done teshuvah?

"I looked into the UFO phenomenon in Israel, and I found that the majority of the sightings had rational explanations, like flares or night-time Air Force training missions, but there were still many unexplained cases, more than any other place. What was so special about Israel and being Jewish? I had to find out more.

"I started taking a few classes, and to make a long story short, I ended up in a yeshivah. Once I started learning, I was delighted to find that a lot of unexplained things in this world — like ghosts, making contact with the dead, magic, and stuff like that — are explained in the Torah. I found a Rashi in Bava Kama (*daf kaf-aleph*) which talks about a haunted house. Yoreh De'ah even talks about a mermaid! But I hardly found anything about UFOs. There's an article by R. Aryeh Kaplan —"

Yossi interjected, "I just read that."

"— and a novel by Hyam Yona Becker. The article didn't say much, and a novel isn't really the thing to help you. And I didn't find anything else. So I was still bothered. I mean, the reports can't all be explained by natural phenomenon, and I find it hard to believe that every photo or eyewitness account is a forgery or a prank. So I kept thinking, 'Based on the evidence, how would the Torah explain the fact that so many people see these things?' In the end I came up with my own explanation. I asked a few

Rabbis about it, and they didn't see anything wrong with it. I was kind of surprised, though, when I told it to some of my friends at the website, and they told me I was crazy. They were convinced aliens were piloting those flying saucers, and wouldn't hear anything else, no matter how logical."

The boys sat in silence.

Simchah went on, "I believe all these UFOs are nothing but personal messages from Hashem. Only the people they're intended for can see them. They can even be photographed. But they're not real. There's nothing really there. They're only images. They're out there only to give you a message. That's why Israel has more per capita than any other country. That's why UFOs don't make a sonic boom. That's why some people see them and others don't, and that's why there are no massive eyewitness reports."

There was silence for a moment, then Baruch shook himself. "From Hashem? Why? What kind of message?"

Simchah leaned forward and placed his hands on his knees. "Don't you guys see it? What's the idea of a UFO? That there's something out there with greater intelligence looking down at us. The slogan of one film was 'We are not alone.' And it's true, too, that we're not alone, only it's Hashem who's always with us.

"In earlier times we had prophets to advise and direct us. Nowadays it's a time of *hester panim*, when God hides His face and acts behind the scenes, so He has to send us messages in roundabout ways."

Yossi was speechless. UFOs are images sent from Hashem? He felt flutters in his heart; he was awe-stricken at the thought that Hashem had given him a personal message. Before he could say anything, Baruch asked, "What was so urgent? Why did we have to see it?"

Simchah's features turned a bit more serious. "You told me," he said very gently, "that you both missed yeshivah on Tuesday to take a hike at Bear Mountain. Why did you cut out from learning Torah to go on a hike?" Both boys froze. Simchah nodded silently. "Had you been doing this sort of thing before?"

Yossi folded his hands and looked at the wall for a few moments, while turning red in the face.

Baruch was the first to speak up. "Well… we missed yeshivah a few weeks ago to go to the Yankee game."

"Why are you guys cutting yeshivah so much?" Simchah asked, being careful to keep his voice gentle.

Yossi finally broke his silence to tell Simchah about his escape to the NBA websites, his loss of interest in learning, and how as a result he was doing poorly in class.

"Did anything cause all this?" asked Simchah. "Did something happen recently to you, or anyone in your family, that turned you off and made you want to run away?"

Yossi sat fidgeting for a few moments, looked at the floor, and whispered, "My uncle."

Simchah raised his eyebrow. "Your uncle? Who's that? What about him?"

Yossi said slowly, "My uncle's name was Tzvi Berger. He was one of the victims in a suicide bombing in Machaneh Yehudah."

Simchah said, "Oh! I know that name. I never knew he

was your uncle."

Simchah could see the hurt look on Yossi's face as he sadly said, "Uncle Tzvi set up an organization to help victims of terror attacks. He raised money for them and had a camp in Switzerland. Even though he worked so hard to help victims of terrorism, he himself became a victim. I don't understand how it could happen."

Simchah nodded a couple of times slowly. "I think I get it. You saw an unjust, undeserved death, and you couldn't understand how the Judge of the World could do that. You didn't find an answer in the *sefarim*, and there was no one to ask. No one to talk to. So you had to run away from the whole business. The Web provided an escape to keep you from thinking. But whenever you weren't logged on, the question kept nagging you, so you couldn't keep your mind on anything, let alone learning — especially since the Torah seemed to have failed, by not giving you the answer you needed."

Yossi's mouth hung open. Finally he managed to ask, "How do you know all that?"

Simchah looked at Yossi with a gentle expression, and said simply, "Been there, done that, got the t-shirt."

"You mean I'm —"

"No, you're not the only one who's suffered from unanswered questions. Nor are you the only one who's suffered from people who don't have the time or the heart to give time and attention. Eventually I found people who would give these, and I got the answers to my questions; you'll get the answers to yours in good time. But the answers don't come easy, and they don't always explain everything. After all, we're only flesh and flood, and there are limits to our understanding.

"I'm not a prophet, but maybe that's the message Hashem wanted to send you: that there are things in this world, like what happened to your uncle, that can't be fully explained. That's what a UFO means to most people: something that no one can rationally define. Maybe that's why Hashem sent you a message in this fashion."

Yossi felt a weight lift off his shoulders. Placing his hands behind him, he leaned back. For the first time in months, he began to relax.

Simchah told the boys, "It seems to be a pattern with people who sight UFO: they've usually just had some sort of traumatic experience. Some skeptics explain away UFOs in just this manner: the person needs a support system so badly, he'll fool himself into thinking he saw a flying saucer to give himself something to believe in. His whole world has been shaken by his bad experience, and now he needs to feel something is 'out there.'" Simchah smiled. "As Jews, we already know it's Hashem who is the one out there."

Simchah now turned to Baruch, who was staring at the ceiling. Why did he suddenly look so nervous? On a hunch he asked, "How have things been going for you in yeshivah, Baruch? How's the learning been?" Baruch flushed and remained silent; Simchah nodded to himself again. "Have you had a death in the family, anything like that?"

"No," Baruch said tentatively.

"So how have your grades been? Come on, work with me. Let's get a handle on things."

"Everything's been fine," he said in a monotone.

Yossi burst in, "That's not what you told me last week. You said you didn't know half the questions on the last Gemara test."

The room fell into an uncomfortable silence. Then Simchah said gently, "If it's true Hashem sent you a message through a UFO, it makes sense to at least try to figure out what the message is, don't you agree?"

Baruch paused for a few moments, then finally said, "Well, I guess it all started a few months ago when I met this guy in a Web chat room. He told me that he keeps *mitzvos*, but he takes one Shabbos off every month. That sounded good, but now that I think about things, it's been downhill since then."

Yossi scratched his head. "A Shabbos off? What's so bad about that? You mean he goes away for that Shabbos?"

Baruch smiled, "I mean that he doesn't observe that Shabbos! He drives his car, goes to the movies, the beach, wherever he wants. Last week he went to a rock concert. He said there's a *heter* in *halachah* for such a thing, only it isn't talked about because the Rabbis don't want anyone to know about it."

Simchah asked, "So you've been talking with him in the chat room about this, and got to thinking about it...."

"What do you mean, 'got to thinking about it'? I've been using that *heter* a lot the past few months. I tell my parents I'm going away for Shabbos, and I do go away, but not to places they would approve of."

Both Yossi and Simchah sat there stunned.

Simchah asked, "I gather your parents don't know what you really do?"

Baruch shot back, "My father's a big Rosh Yeshivah. If he found out, he'd throw me out of the house."

Simchah said quietly, "Why wait for him to find out? Why not ask him straight out about this supposed *heter?* He'd tell you it's all nonsense. You could learn it up with him and see the *emess* together."

Baruch shifted uncomfortably. "I don't talk to my father very much. He's got no time for me. If he's not preparing a *shiur,* he's on the phone about an important cause, or he's working out the latest fund-raising plan to save his yeshivah."

"Your father doesn't make any time for you?"

"With eleven kids, how can he?" Baruch shot back. Then he mumbled, "Anyway, he doesn't seem too interested in me."

Simchah leaned back by the computer desk, a distant look in his eyes. He was staring into his own past, and thinking painfully, "Why? All these kids who have a home and a family, and yet they don't. Why?" After a few seconds he pulled himself together, leaned forward in the chair, and looked straight at Baruch. "God doesn't tell me why He does what He does," he said, "but I just thought of something. You're pretty upset that your father doesn't give you attention, but look what happened on Tuesday. Your Father in Heaven took out some time to send you a special message. One that nobody else in the whole world, except for Yossi, saw. Hashem obviously has faith in you, and hasn't given up on you, or else why would He send it?

Maybe it was a sign to give up this 'off-Shabbos' nonsense."

Baruch sat there with a blank look on his face. He'd never considered himself important enough for anyone, least of all God, to take an interest in his life. Finally he mumbled, "This is all so weird. I mean, they didn't see flying saucers a hundred years ago. If God wanted to send me a message, why didn't my grandfather come to me in a dream or something? I mean, he was a big *tzaddik*."

Simchah shrugged. "Each generation has its needs, and they're always different than what previous ones needed. What worked in the *shtetl* won't necessarily work nowadays. It's a different generation, and with it come new challenges. Hashem sends us wake-up calls in all kinds of different forms." After all, he thought privately, if the parents don't care, it's up to our Father in Heaven to care.

"I still haven't bought the idea," said Baruch, "that Hashem was sending me a special message."

Simchah replied on the spot: "Look, you did see something nobody else in the world saw except for Yossi, right? So, even if you want to believe that aliens were piloting that flying saucer, it still wouldn't change the fact that Hashem is sending you a message. It was there, after all.

"For some people the message has to be sent through sickness, for others through some other tragedy. Still others Hashem trusts better, and He sends them a less painful message, even a weird one like a flying saucer. I think Hashem wanted to talk to both of you at the same time, and He did it in the form of a flying saucer, so you'd have free will to decide for yourself what it meant."

Baruch slowly stood up from the bed. Yossi noticed his eyebrows knitted. For the first time in months he had a serious expression on his face. He firmly said, "Okay. No more of these off-Shabboses."

"Right your are. And look, if you feel you need to get away or you need someone to talk to, you can call me anytime. I always have time to talk with guys in your situation."

Baruch smiled and said, "Let me take down your number."

Afterwards the three went down to the kitchen for some hot chocolate. In the more relaxed setting, Yossi told Simchah about what went on after they had seen the UFO, about the ice-cream vendor and the park ranger and the others. Simchah related some of the cases he'd worked with, and how the person had often turned his life around after seeing a UFO. After about an hour, Simchah looked at his watch and said, "I really have to get going. I've got a long ride back to Queens." He looked at Baruch and asked, "Do you need a lift to your house?"

Baruch smiled. "No thanks. I need to catch up in the Gemara. I'm going to ask Mendy if he'll go over it with us tonight."

Simchah walked to the door and thought, "Learning on Motzaei Shabbos? I guess they learned something else from UFOs. They both move quickly."

also by Zev Roth...

Two towns in two countries with at least one thing in common: great stories! Ordinary people in extraordinary circumstances, people who discovered Torah in unexpected ways, and more. Forty stories, all fascinating, all absolutely true. 224 pp.

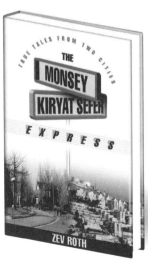

Zev Roth does it again! 30 more unusual, exciting and absolutely true stories that take you to Monsey, Kiryat Sefer, and every point in between. 224 pp.

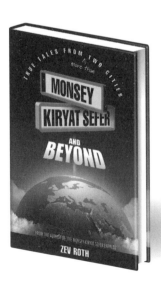

now available from TARGUM PRESS

OR ORDER ON-LINE AT WWW.TARGUM.COM